THE COURIER

A LAWSON VAMPIRE MISSION #6

JON F. MERZ

Copyright © 2005/2019 by Jon F. Merz

All rights reserved.

No part of this book may be reproduced in any form or by any electronic or mechanical means, including information storage and retrieval systems, without written permission from the author, except for the use of brief quotations in a book review.

DISCLAIMER

This is a work of fiction. Names, characters, businesses, places, events and incidents are either the products of the author's imagination or used in a fictitious manner. Any resemblance to actual persons, living or dead, or actual events is purely coincidental.

THE PRICE OF A GOOD DRINK
A LAWSON VAMPIRE STORY #5

"Used to be," said the man behind the bar drying shot glasses, "you could tell the man by the type of drink he ordered."

He slapped the towel he'd been using over his shoulder. It must have been a sharp white once, like the snow before it touches the filth in the city. But years of use had worn it down to a dull ecru color. I could see tattered threads squiggling their way out of the stitch patterns, hanging loose in the air, waiting to be unraveled even more.

In front of me, the glass of Bombay Sapphire and tonic sat untouched. I watched the wedge of lime loll midway between the surface and the bottom of the glass. Every now and again, I'd use the stirrer to send it flying through the liquid and ice like it was in a zero-gravity environment. It would bounce off one side and then head back the way it had come.

Sometimes I'm really easy to entertain.

Off in the distance, the Beatles crooned about Strawberry Fields. I thought about how much I used to dig the Beatles. Before they got lost in their hallucinogenic drug phase and became preachers for a kinder gentler world. In my book, the world's already got plenty of people who preach. What we need is a few more deeds.

I glanced up at the bartender. He was eyeing me. Waiting for me to come back at him with some response. I wasn't really feeling talkative, but the day was dark with rain clouds pissing down the kind of drizzle that seems to seep into everywhere, even if you've got yourself a raincoat or an umbrella. My mood felt about the same.

"Not anymore?" Two words wouldn't kill me.

He leaned against the bar and shook his head. "Nah. Got too many fancy drinks these days. Damned things crop up faster than zits on a teenager. I can't even remember all the names."

"I know some of them. They sound like vacation getaways."

"Exactly." He shook his head. "Back when I was first learning how to pour, it was simple stuff. Whiskey, bourbon, scotch, gin. Draft beers. Maybe a glass of wine for the ladies. That was it."

"You been around that long?"

He tried to grin around the burden of memories he looked like he was carrying. "Days like this, it feels like forever."

I knew the feeling. Lately my own life had felt like a record that kept skipping in place over a refrain I didn't want to sing anymore. "Maybe you should open your own place."

"No chance. I've never had a head for business. But I'm a damned good barkeep. I know my trade. And yeah, even those silly fruity drinks the kids want. I can pour with the best of them."

"But you long for the old days."

He came off the rail and nodded. "How's that drink?"

I sipped it, tasting the way the licorice and juniper came together to form what I thought was the world's greatest gin. The flavors rolled over my tongue. I caught some of the lime – tart and welcoming amid the thicker liquor.

"Damned good," I said after the swallow.

He nodded like I just told him he was savior of mankind. "I figured you for one of the old guys."

"Old guys?"

"Yeah. A man who knows how to drink a drink. Hell, a man who knows how to order one. You don't try to impress. It's the same with the drink. A good drink never tries to impress anyone. It just is. You know that the moment you sip it for the first time. It's got its own confidence. Its own demeanor."

The place was almost empty. A booth in the back held two guys who were huddled together, probably discussing the next Internet revolution. I noticed the expensive Burberry coats they wore. The briefcases on the floor. Their shoes.

Another guy lounged down near the end of the bar nursing a draft beer that looked more like a urine sample than anything else. I figured it for one of those stupid new low-carb light beers that supposedly satisfies the craving without ever really doing so.

I grinned at the barkeep. "Now don't go making me out to be something I'm not."

"I don't have to. You already are."

If he'd only known. The list of friends I'd been burying lately. The list of enemies that seemed to grow longer with each passing minute. The weight of a personal destiny that I sometimes couldn't stand to shoulder.

"I just want a quick drink."

"Nothing quick about a drink like that. You're doing some thinking. I know it. I can see it in your eyes."

He was right. Sitting in the airport bar waiting for my flight to leave for Japan, I figured the booze would help ease my mind some. Maybe even take the edge off. Fourteen-hour plane rides aren't my usual bag. But a trip to Japan was precisely what I needed right now. Especially if I had any hope of continuing my work as a Fixer.

"A bartender's wisdom?"

"I've seen everything, man. You know what I mean?"

"Guess so."

"Most people, you know they wouldn't believe working a joint like this would grant them those all-seeing eyes. But it does. Somethings, well they're easy to make out. You can spot the guy who's just gotten dumped. You can spot the jilted lover or the lady who walks in on her man screwing the bejeezuz out of some take-out club slut."

"Colorful."

He ignored me. "But the other things? Sometimes they're tougher to notice. But they're there anyway. Just because the vast majority of people can't notice the end of their nose to save their lives doesn't mean those things don't exist. People who come in here – they've got blinders on bad. Real bad."

"Cellphones are the bane of society."

"Not just them. It's other stuff. Computers, advertisements, TV, movies, music. It's this rush world we live in that makes people unable to see the things that are right in front of them."

"Anyone ever tell you you sound a little like that Unabomber fellow?"

He grinned but it came out...sad almost. "I don't want to blow anything up. I've got no desire to see anyone get killed."

"Probably a good thing. Mankind doesn't seem to need any more help in that regard."

I sipped the drink and waited for him to say something. He didn't. I glanced up and found him eyeballing me again.

I hefted the glass. "Drink's good."

He blinked and walked away from me. Good old Lawson the conversation killer. Chalk another one up on the list of people who think I suck in a royal way. I took another sip of gin and listened as the Beatles mercifully finished whining and Rush took over the lead with "Red Alert." The bartender must have had it tuned to WZLX, which was Boston's classic rock station and the only one that would have paired two unlikely bands like that. I didn't mind much, though since I happened to dig Rush. They were one of the bands I'd only recently started appreciating.

My foot started tapping in time to the beat. I took another sip, listened to a clap of thunder break out somewhere above my head, and saw the windows melt under a fresh assault of withering rain.

Great day for a flight.

My timing had sucked lately and it just didn't seem to be getting any better. Getting back from New York, I'd found myself in the dumps. I'm not usually much on self-pity, but I could tell I was worn out. Fighting the Syndicate and trying to figure out who was still out there pulling the strings to some of the most insidious corruption I'd ever stumbled across, had exhausted me beyond what a couple of beers and a Patriots football game could cure.

I thought about Teresa and how I'd left her in that old resort up in Mohunk. How her eyes had gone so deep black as her pupils had finally dilated as she died. I could remember feeling how cold she'd gone when the evil midget Cho had stuck her with a couple of hypodermics full of his new designer drug Saber.

Teresa'd been a casualty of war. My war. She'd been an innocent that I'd gotten caught up in the affairs of the vampire world. She was someplace no human should have ever been. And it was my fault she was dead.

I was supposed to be out there protecting people and here I was getting them killed. No one would ever shed much of a tear over Teresa. None of my superiors would care as long as her death didn't threaten the Balance. They could live with her death no problem.

I wondered if I could.

"Still deep in thought?"

I glanced up and found the bartender back in front of me. "I thought I killed any trace of conversation."

"I've got other customers."

I looked around. The two Internet geniuses were still huddled in the back booth. They must have been discussing something really absorbing because neither of their glasses looked like they'd been touched. The guy at the end of the bar stared into the foamy depths of his beer stein and took a hefty pull on it before thunking it down again.

The place was dead.

"Don't let me keep you from anything."

He frowned and moved off to the other end of the bar to fill the guy's mug with a fresh draft. All the while, he kept staring at me. Frankly, I was getting a little tired of it.

I sipped my drink some more. Alcohol wasn't exactly a prescription for lifting my spirits. Damned stuff made you even more depressed. Truth was, I wasn't even sure if I wanted my spirits elevated. Sometimes, a good funk is just the kick in the ass you need to get moving again.

Or maybe I was changing. Maybe I was becoming one of those folks who needs the dozen or so prescription tablets I saw advertised ad nauseam on the evening news every night while I was trying to enjoy my dinner without thinking about heartburn, allergies, erectile dysfunction or my toe nails falling off.

Jesus Christ.

If things kept looking as dim as that, I'd save a bullet for myself and just be done with it. Easier than dragging it out. I think that was big problem with smokers in general. In my eyes, it was suicide. Sure, they're dragging it out for years, but they're killing themselves anyway. Wouldn't it be better to just do it fast and get it over with? Cripes, at least I could muster some respect for them then. A little courage of conviction goes a long way with me.

Cynical bastard.

Behind the bar, my own eyes stared back at me in the mirrored glass. Someone had told me that once. That I was too cynical. I told them I was cynical because of all the hopeless and pathetic shit I'd seen traipsing around this damned planet in pursuit of some higher ideal that I wasn't so sure I wanted to be a part of.

Then I kicked him in the balls.

Merry Christmas, sunshine. Don't want me to be cynical? How about showing me why? I could use a little proof of why I should give a shit if my mood pissed someone off. I could stand seeing just a speck of brightness in this dreary-ass world where everyone was out for themselves and no one seemed to give a rat's ass if you got screwed in the process.

Terrorism? Wars? Religious extremism? It all boiled down to someone manipulating other people so they could line their own pockets. It came down to greed, plain and simple. People could scream all they wanted that they were doing things in the interest of their fellow man, but it was all bullshit. All it took was a set of eyes unbiased enough to see through the fog. Look deep enough and everyone boiled down to the least common denominator of 'selfish prick.'

"Need a refill?"

I sighed. "I'm not done yet."

"Figured maybe those ice cubes were starting to water down the drink."

I nodded at the glasses behind the bar. "You're looking for something to do, some of those puppies back there look a bit smudged."

"Grumpy bastard, aren't you?"

I grinned. "You're bowling me over with that cry-on-my-shoulder-bartender routine."

"You should see me when I get annoyed."

"I'm not in the mood."

He shrugged. "Funny thing about being annoyed. It doesn't always let you choose the time and place, you know?"

"I know a lot of things like that."

"I'll bet you do." He slapped his towel down on the bar. "Where you off to, anyway?"

"Japan."

"No shit?"

"Not that I can see."

He smirked. "Why would you go over there?"

I swirled some more of the drink around my mouth. He might have been right about the ice cubes. "The simplest answer of all."

"Yeah?"

"There ain't here."

"You running from something?"

I nudged the glass toward him. "A watery drink right now."

He poured me a fresh one and slid it back. "Anything else?"

"You don't have enough Bombay Sapphire back there to last how long it would take me to go down the list."

"That long?" He mopped the bar with the towel and slung it over his shoulder.

I shrugged. "We're not talking about a thirty-second news bite."

"So you came in here to lose yourself?"

I looked at him again. Harder this time. "I came in here for a drink. Nothing more."

The towel came down on the bar again. "I wonder how many people would ever ask a bartender if his life was all a bed of roses."

"Probably not many."

"They don't care, that's what it is." He leaned back and sighed. "I've heard so many goddamned sob stories from the whiniest bunch of losers on the planet. Sometimes it makes me sick."

I was considering being offended at the whiny bunch of losers comment, but let it pass. The drink was good, after all. "Only sometimes?"

"Sometimes you enjoy it. It gives you a different perspective on your own life. Makes you appreciate all the good things you have."

"I guess."

"Like only recently. This guy comes in sits down about where you're sitting right now and lays down the worst story I ever heard. I mean really bust-your-balls shit. Like it was either something good happened in the next few minutes or people were going to die."

"That bad?"

"Yep."

I glanced down the bar again to see if the bartender's story had piqued the curiosity of any of the other guys. None of them showed any interest. The guy down the bar seemed to be having trouble staying awake.

I looked back at the bartender. "So, what was the story?"

"Comes in this guy, and says to me, 'you know what it's like to not know if you're going to be alive in the next few minutes?'"

"Helluvan opener. Did he say he used it to get laid or not?"

"I don't think he did. It'd scare off the chicks."

"Probably." Although I knew one or two who might have found that pretty damned alluring.

"So I says to him I says, 'Buddy, you want a drink or what?' and he looks back at me and says, 'just one because I've got a gun.'"

"Lucky you getting a poet like that."

"I asked him why he had a gun and he told me he was going to get two of his friends and hold the airport hostage."

"The whole airport?" I smiled. "Three guys to one airport. The numbers don't exactly add up."

"That's what I thought, but this guy, he don't look like that kind of thing bothers him all that much. I got the feeling he was having a drink to celebrate his imminent demise."

"So what this guy looked like a terrorist?"

"He wasn't Muslim. Didn't look like a convert from behind bars, either, the way some of them blacks fall in with the Nation of Islam and shit. Come out reborn and with those long-ass names I could never spell right."

"Lotta folks find religion in jail. Keeps them from getting raped."

"And there are no atheists in a foxhole. Yeah, I heard that before."

"So this was a white guy? Average Joe?"

"Yeah."

"With a gun."

"Uh huh."

"And two pals?"

"Well, they come in a little later. Didn't look like him, either. They looked professional like. Business suits and stuff. Maybe it was part of their disguise."

"So this guy talks to them when they came in? Them being friends and all?"

"Nope. Not a word passed between them. Like they didn't want to acknowledge the other existed. Weird, huh?"

"Well, I wouldn't call it weird. A little screwy sure, but not the worst story caliber you just played down on me."

"But it gets worse."

I nursed my drink. I could feel the gin working overtime to

ease my pain. It didn't help that it took a lot more alcohol to get me drunk than it did for normal humans. I'd have to have a few more of these before I felt the pain going away. Of course, the way the bartender was telling his story, that might not have been much of an issue.

"So go on already."

"This guy he drinks his first beer and then tells me that unfortunately, because he told me the plan, he was going to have to kill me."

"No shit."

"Yeah. How's that for a kicker?"

"Not what you want to hear at work."

"Exactly. Infidelity, bad bosses, bankruptcy, dead dogs, that's what you hear about. Finding out I was going to be killed wasn't on that list."

"I imagine I'd pour myself a glass of something from back there if I heard that."

"Yeah, that's what I wanted to do."

"How come you didn't?"

"Another customer came in. I had to serve him instead."

I hefted my drink in his direction. "Well, here's to you staying alive."

"Day ain't over yet."

"Well, it's obvious the guy didn't fulfill his objective. The place is fine. Airport's standing just as she ever was. And unless I'm sadly mistaken, you are still very much alive."

The bartender just looked at me with that sad kind of look I've seen teachers save for the kids who just don't get it. The guy probably had me riding the short bus to school in his mind.

"Maybe I was wrong about you."

I finished off my drink. "Could be. I haven't exactly been fulfilling a lot of people's expectations about me lately."

Somewhere between the gin and my melancholy mood, a

tiny piece of my subconscious started buzzing. I frowned and started to look up when I heard the telltale click of the hammer being pulled back on a pistol.

My eyes shifted right. The barrel loomed like some giant black hole ready to suck in the life of everything around it.

The almost-asleep nobody from down the bar seemed pretty awake now. And steady. The way he held the gun told me he was no slouch with it, either. I could see the determination set in his jaw.

"Nice little tale you had going there, asshole."

The bartender shrugged. "Can't blame a guy for trying."

"Oh sure I can." The pistol turned, coughed once and a bright bloom of red sprayed the front of the bartender's shirt. He crashed to the ground and lay still. I could smell the smoke issuing out of the end of the gun. I figured any minute now the door to the bar would crash open and all these heavily armed state troopers would pour in with their MP5s and hose this dude down.

That didn't happen.

"Too noisy out there for them to hear one shot." He lowered the gun slightly and I felt okay about turning my head to look at him.

"So, what's your beef?"

"No beef."

"You just woke up today and decided you wanted to cause death and mayhem?" I grinned. "And I used to think I was impulsive."

In the back, the two businessmen slid out of the booth and wandered over to the bar. They hefted their briefcases up onto the mahogany and clicked them open. From inside they took out two Skorpion machine pistols. Close-in, those things were awful. They handled them like professionals.

My drink was empty and I wasn't particularly thrilled with

my present company. "So, this is it, huh? You three ride out to do battle with what...the infidels?"

"You think this is about Islamic extremism?" said Sleepy.

"Isn't that the popular fad these days?"

"There are other reasons for doing what we're doing."

"That so?"

One of the briefcase jockeys looked at Sleepy and frowned. "He doesn't need to know."

"What difference does it make? Another forty seconds he'll be dead anyway."

I hefted my empty glass. "He's right. Without a fresh one, I've got no real reason for living."

Sleepy leaned forward. "It's a war, man. No other way around it. We've got to do what we're going to do because no one else is going to do it."

"But why?"

"Because we're being invaded."

My eyebrows waggled some the way they normally did when I thought I might be talking to a lunatic or a close relative of one. "By who? Canada? Mexico?"

Sleepy cast his eyes around. "No. We're being invaded from within. By evil creatures."

"Creatures."

"Yeah."

"What kind of creatures?"

He looked at me. "You'll think I'm crazy."

"Too late for that, Sunshine. C'mon already. Your forty seconds are almost up."

"You mean your forty seconds."

"That's one way of looking at it."

He stepped back. "All right hotshot. How about this: we're being invaded by vampires."

That stopped me. But only for a moment. I knew there were

enough crazy idiots out there who thought themselves vampires and would have jumped at perpetrating a rumor like that. Sleepy might have had a bad encounter at a Goth nightclub, for crying out loud.

"Vampires."

"Yeah. But not like the ones we read about. These ones are real."

"You think there are vampires invading the country?"

"They're taking over from within. They drink blood, yeah, but they don't need coffins and shit like that. They can walk around in daylight."

"You realize that sounds completely insane."

"It's the truth man."

"And you're going to do what with those guns exactly?"

"Go outside and shoot everyone we can see."

"Uh…"

He cut me off. "The ones who get up after we shoot them are obviously vampires. That will be the proof we need to convince the authorities we aren't crazy. The video cameras in the terminal will catch the whole thing."

"Interesting." They might have been nuts but there was an uncomfortable logic to their plan. Statistically speaking, the vampire population wasn't all that big in Boston. But they might get real lucky and stumble across one.

After all, they'd already been fortunate enough to come across one dumbass.

"It'll work, too," said Sleepy. "You'll see." He caught himself. "Well, no, I guess you won't." He stepped back further and leveled the pistol at my head. "Guess your time's up, pal."

I glanced at my watch. "Actually, it expired about ten seconds ago."

Sleepy thumbed the hammer back on his piece. "See you on the other side."

I smiled. "Ladies first." And slapped the barrel out of the way with my left hand as I came off my stool and then sent my right fist into Sleepy's trachea. The gun went off with a boom, exploding several bottles of Southern Comfort behind the bar. No waste there; I hate that shit.

Sleepy sank on his knees gagging out of control. He was out of the fight for now but I had the Skorpion Twins to worry about now.

They might have handled guns like pros but they weren't used to being in battle. They moved in slow time, reacting out of surprise rather than instinct. Their guns came up too slow and I was able to get one in front of the other, using the middle as cover.

A steady chop-chop-chop buzzed the air as the rear Twin unleashed his piece on full-auto. The middle Twin never stood a chance. His insides got chainsawed.

I kept moving around to the left side of the bar, grabbing my empty glass with one hand, crashing it down on the bar and feeling the bite of broken glass slice into my hand. The surging adrenaline in my system dulled the pain.

The last Twin ran out of bullets and came at me rather than try to reload. I gave him points for that. Unfortunately, I also gave him the jagged edge of my empty glass in his eye socket as he closed with me.

He screamed and clutched at his eye. Too late, I moved behind him, grabbed his jaw and jerked it to one side. His neck popped twice and he stopped screaming. I let him slip to the floor.

Sleepy was still gagging. His face looked a little blue and I supposed the lack of oxygen would shortly render him unconscious before he died.

I knelt beside him. "You picked the wrong bar today, pal."

His eyes widened as I picked up his gun. Maybe he thought I was going to shoot him with it.

I leaned closer. "Who told you about the vampires?"

He shrugged an 'I don't know' and went back to trying to gag himself some more air. I could see his eyes. He looked about ready to check out.

I made the decision in a split-second. Maybe I was feeling a little punchy today after all. I let my canines extend and then smiled at Sleepy.

"You were right, you know. We do exist."

Whatever final shred of consciousness Sleepy possessed made sense of my teeth and his eyes grew even wider. Then he passed out. He'd be dead in another two minutes.

I walked behind the bar and got myself a fresh glass. The bartender was still dead and I didn't think he'd mind all that much anyway. I poured another dollop of Bombay Sapphire into my glass, added some tonic water, ice, and a wedge of lime that I squeezed into the mix. I stirred it with my finger and drank.

Humans knowing about vampires didn't sit all that well with me. It was my job to make sure that kind of knowledge didn't come to be widespread. But someone out there knew about us.

I wondered if maybe the Syndicate had something to do with it.

The sudden appearance of four heavily armed State Troopers with MP5s at ready derailed my train of thought. They burst through the door. I stopped moving.

"Freeze!"

The lead guy came ahead and quickly figured out the scene. He glanced at me. "You took out three guys?"

I took another sip of my drink. "Crazy luck."

"Damn fool, more likely."

"No argument from me."

He surveyed the scene some more. "We'll need some information and a statement."

I slid him my passport. "Here's the info. My statement is this: I was sitting here having a drink when those three hauled out the hardware, screamed something about being invaded by aliens, blasted the bartender and then made to kill me. I took out the guy with the pistol first and then two other two pretty much did each other."

"That's it?"

I held up my hands. "Does it look like there's anything else?"

"Guess not." He eyed my passport and made some notes on his notebook. "You going to be around if we need some more information from you?"

"Nope."

"No?"

"I'm headed to Japan."

"Coming back?"

I looked at the bar and the three guys who thought they were going to save the human race by exposing vampires to the world. That kind of fanaticism didn't make me feel so good.

"Yeah. I'll be back." I took the final gulp of my drink and slammed my glass back down on the bar. From my pocket I took out a twenty dollar bill and left it under the glass.

The State Trooper looked at it. "I don't think anyone'll mind if you skip out on the bill."

"Probably not. But I'll leave it just the same."

He pointed at the corpses. "A job like this, maybe someone ought to be paying you."

I started for the door. "Money's overrated."

"You kidding me?"

I leaned against the door and pushed it open slightly. Outside, I could hear the bustle of the terminal. I could see the faces of the curious trying to get a glimpse inside the bar at the bloodshed. They stared at me. Wondered who the hell I was. What the hell I had done that I could just walk out of there like no one's business.

I glanced back at the cop. "Sometimes, it just takes a good drink to make it all worthwhile."

"You're a strange dude, you know that?"

I smiled but I didn't feel all that jolly. "I've got a plane to catch.." Outside, I tried to lose myself in the barrage of human travelers. But already, I knew some of my precious anonymity had been lost.

And I wasn't sure any drink was worth that price.

THE COURIER

A LAWSON VAMPIRE MISSION #6

1

As many times as I've stared down the barrel of a gun, I never get cocky about it.

Well, that's not entirely true. Sometimes I've been pretty damned snarky.

But something about the peculiar rifling of this barrel made me think twice about letting loose with my usual snide commentary. I chose to recall how less than an hour ago, the only thought in my head was that I was supposed to be in Japan.

Instead, I had dragged my tired ass through the customs line at Manila International Airport, trying my best to reach my Control Niles back in Boston to let him know about my unannounced and unplanned diversion. For some reason, I'd fallen asleep halfway across the Pacific when we were still bound for Tokyo and woken up a few thousand miles closer to the equator.

Cardboard boxes the size of washing machines surrounded me. People dragged them everywhere. The luggage claim area spat them out one after another, all wrapped with bits of string and taped up to strengthen corners and seams. I gave my passport to the control officer and nodded at the boxes.

"What the hell are those things?"

"Balikbayang. 'Going home boxes.' Filipinos use them to transport goods when they travel."

"You guys don't believe in suitcases?"

He grinned. "Not big enough." He studied my charming frown in the passport photo and looked back at me. "How long are you here for, Mr. Lawson?"

"Twenty-four hours. Long enough to figure out why I'm not in Japan - where I should be - and get a flight there."

He nodded and stamped me in. "Well, have a nice stay. There's a restaurant around the corner that serves a great palabo."

I had no idea what palabo was but I wasn't in the mood for a culinary lesson. "Thanks."

My own bag was significantly smaller than the cardboard boxes people lugged everywhere. I stowed it in a locker, pulled out the key and headed toward the front of the terminal building. People rammed into each other, doing a bad imitation of a demolition derby. No one apologized. No one said excuse me. I thought about body checking my way to the front of the line but decided diplomacy might be the better option. At least for now.

The doors slid open and I walked outside smack into a wall of heavy, wet heat.

"Cripes."

The door closed behind me and I stood there, feeling an instant sweat come on. Welcome to the jungle. I was dressed for moderate weather. This time of year in Japan, the temperatures would be pleasant but possibly cool at night.

I wasn't dressed for the tropics.

My cell phone buzzed in my pocket. I flipped it open and saw the name attached to the number. "Niles."

"Hi Lawson."

"Do you have any idea where I am right now?"

"Of course I do. You're probably standing just outside the

main terminal door at Manila International Airport wondering if you should go back inside and figure things out or stay on the curb sweating for no good reason."

I paused. Niles was as good a Control as I've ever had. When I first met him, I thought he was a flake but he proved himself a number of times to be steady and resolute in the heat of battle. Plus, he had my back, something I always value.

But even I had no idea how the hell he knew I was in the Philippines and told him so.

"You ordered a glass of orange juice while your flight was over the Bering Sea, right?"

"Yeah…"

"Flight attendant slipped a little something into it. Sort of guaranteed you wouldn't wake up when the plane touched down in Japan."

I frowned. "She was one of us?"

"Yep."

"And why, exactly, wouldn't I want to be awake when we touched down in Japan? I mean, I'm supposed to be heading there on vacation. Right?"

"You will be, trust me. It's just I need you to do a quick favor."

"In the Philippines."

"Right."

I sighed. My shirt was soaked through and felt like a clammy second layer of skin. One I wanted to molt as soon as possible. "You're telling me there are no active Fixers working this side of the Pacific?"

"None who could pull this job off as well as you can."

"I appreciate the flattery, Niles, but stop championing me as the savior of our race. It gets me more assignments than I can handle."

"This one's quick. I promise."

A flatbed handcart loaded with balikbayang came trundling

toward me at high speed. I dodged it as a little old lady wheeled it past. "If I die here, I'm coming back to haunt you as a giant refrigerator box."

"I'm not even going to ask what that means."

I sighed. "What's the job?"

"Remember Vienna in '84?"

"Like a bad tequila hangover. Please tell me this doesn't have anything to do with that."

A burst of intercontinental static fizzled in my ear, but I heard Niles all the same. "Sorry, pal."

Vienna had gone down as one of the nastiest assignments I'd ever dealt with. Traitors, a conspiracy, and even me coming face-to-face with lycanthropes for the first time. I wasn't crazy about revisiting that portion of my past.

"More werewolves?"

"Not so far. But there's memory chip containing the latest information on our Fixer networks – names, faces, locations, Controls, even Loyalists – all on a keychain-sized flash memory drive."

I needed sunglasses soon or I was going to go blind in the seething sunlight. "It's here?"

"Due to touch down within twenty-four hours. We lost the courier somewhere between New York and Washington. He was jumping planes, paying cash for short range flights, doing anything to lose surveillance and make it tough to track him via computer."

"But he's coming here. How do you know?"

Niles cleared his throat. "We set up a sting."

I nodded. "Cool. Who's the buyer?"

"You are, pal."

I looked at my arms. My skin's a mix of my German and Italian heritage. I burn first and then tan up nicely. But I hadn't been sun bathing since last summer. I was as pasty pale as the silly legends of old painted my kind.

"Yeah, that's going to fly real well. He'll take one look at me and know I just got here, too."

"Doesn't matter. As soon as he shows the goods, it's a done deal."

"A done deal."

"Yeah. Get the flash drive back. Find out where he got it in the first place. And then, uh...deal with him."

"You mean kill him."

There was a pause on the phone. "You know what I mean."

I grinned. For some reason, Niles had a tough time reconciling that part of his job, which was to basically give me my targets and assignments and then step out of the way long enough for me to do my job.

"Just giving you a hard time, Niles."

"Get it done, Lawson. Then you can go off to Japan."

"How am I going to find this guy, anyway?"

"You don't. He'll be looking for you at the Robinson Galleria hotel in Makati. Seat yourself in the bar and wear a ballpoint pen in your breast pocket. He'll make the approach."

I clicked the phone off and stood there for another moment in the blazing solar furnace. I'd never been to the Philippines before, and the weather was rapidly making me wish I'd never left the airport. But a job was a job and if I had to do this in order to get some time to myself in Japan, then so be it.

I retrieved my bag from the locker and slid back outside. First, I had to get to Makati. I walked toward the cabstand, which looked more like a used car lot, full of every misbegotten automobile model that never made it to the United States or Europe, but somehow got dumped here instead.

As I approached, a sleek yellow Ford rolled up and the window came down. "You need a cab, mister?"

I slid into the back seat. Mercifully, the cab had air conditioning and the cool air began drying me out. "Robinson Galleria in Makati."

He nodded and slid the car out onto the pockmarked road that surrounded the airport. Thousands of cars clogged the streets. I'd seen traffic like this is Medellin, Colombia, but this was even worse.

"How long before we get there?"

The cabbie grinned. "The hotel is only about two miles from here. But probably we will be there in about an hour."

"Two miles? An hour? You're joking."

The cabbie shook his head. "Rush hour now. Everyone is heading home. You could walk if you want, but in this heat..."

"I'd cook." I glanced out of the window. "Does everyone here own a car?"

"More than one. A few years ago, the government mandated that license plates with certain numbers could only be driven on certain days. To get around that, the citizens simply went out and purchased other cars with different license plates. Depending on the day, they will drive whichever car has the permitted license plate on it."

"Swell." I didn't even want to know what kind of smog problem they had in Manila if that was the case.

"Are you staying in town long?"

"Just a quick layover."

He nodded again. The cab eased forward. I heard car horns blasting off.

"Is everyone here normally so horny?"

He laughed. "We communicate with our horns. That last toot let the other guy know he could proceed."

"Fascinating." But it really wasn't. I was tired and only slowly recovering from the heat. All I really wanted to do was get to the hotel, meet this clown and kill him and then get the hell out of this frying pan of a country before my skin bubbled off my bones.

We inched forward in the traffic. This was getting me nowhere fast and I worried that the radiator might overheat if we didn't start moving at least ten miles an hour. "You know any shortcuts?"

The cabbie grinned. "Always a shortcut. You want me to take it?"

"Please. Anything is better than this."

He jerked the steering wheel and the car shot down an alley that couldn't have been any wider than ten feet across. The side of the car skimmed the walls on either side with maybe an inch of space. Whoever the cabbie was, he certainly knew how to drive.

We crashed through the alley and emerged into a network of twists and turns, a maze of ghetto slums with trash piled high in heaps, clothes draped over rusted iron railings, and small children scampering for cover.

"Try not to hit the kids, please."

"They'll be beggars if they aren't already. No one would miss them if they got hit."

I leaned forward in my seat. "If you hurt any of them, I'll be upset.."

He shrugged. "Fine. Hang on, please."

The cab jerked sideways again and we shot down another dark alley toward what looked like a dead end. I braced for the impact, but at the last second, the cab shot right nearly perpendicular to the brick wall and we were down another alley. It reminded me of a dirtier Hong Kong. This was the kind of scenery I saw on TV back home when the child sponsorship commercials used to come on right when I was eating dinner.

The cab took five minutes of back routes before we finally came to an abrupt screeching halt.

Around us, the tenements loomed in.

The place was deserted.

"If this is the hotel, I'm really going to have to talk to my travel agent."

The cabbie turned in his seat.

He smiled.

But the gun he aimed at my chest didn't really seem funny.

"Time for us to have a talk, Mr. Lawson."

For a guy who'd only just picked me up a few minutes earlier, he seemed to know an awful lot about me. That didn't exactly make me feel all warm and fuzzy.

And neither did the gun.

2

"Would you mind pointing that the other way?" I smiled when I said it, hoping it might work. I've used this line about a thousand times since I started protecting the secret existence of vampires.

So far, it's never worked.

This was no exception. The cabbie thumbed back the hammer instead.

"No."

"Can't blame a guy for asking." I looked around. "So, what happens now? You going to kill me?"

I already knew the answer. If he'd been sent to kill me, there'd already be a chunk of wood in my chest causing that severe allergic reaction I like to call death. But he hadn't fired the gun yet, so that meant he was here for another reason. That was good news for me.

But bad for him.

"Why are you here?"

I looked at him. The trouble with my race is it's always damned difficult trying to figure out who is and who isn't a vampire. Sure there's a mottled patch of skin down around the clavicle that looks more like a birthmark than anything else, but otherwise, that's about all you have to go on. If you happen to see one of us drinking down a bit of blood courtesy of the global blood bank network that keeps us in the juice, the you might know.

But there's little else to go on unless you shoot someone in the chest with a wooden-tipped bullet and their canines suddenly extend as they buy a ticket for the dinner cruise down the River Styx.

I currently didn't have a weapon since I'd just been on a plane for the better part of a day. Human security types tend to get a wee bit uppity when you start hauling pistols and extra mags full of ammo on jets.

Go figure.

That left shooting the cabbie an unlikely proposition. At least until I got tired of staring at the gun and took it away from him. Which, given my current agitated state of mind, I figured might happen in less than a minute.

"My plane got detoured. I'm hanging out until I can get back to Japan."

He smirked. "You lie."

"Actually, I'm not. I really did get detoured. Trust me, this is the last place I want to be. And sitting here with that thing pointing at me is really not what blows my skirt up."

"Your name is Lawson. You are a Fixer. Sent here to kill someone. I want to know who you were sent to kill."

Cabbie was showing his cards and I didn't like the deck they'd been dealt from. If I could have signaled the Pit Boss over, I would have asked for a new shoe. My bad luck I had to play by the house rules.

"I don't know his name."

The cabbie's eyes widened. "I did not expect you to be so honest."

I shrugged. "Seems as though you know plenty about me. What's the use denying it?"

"Still, I thought it was against your code of honor to admit that you are a Fixer."

"Well, yeah ordinarily. I mean if you were going to be alive in the next minute, I might not have told you anything." I leaned right and slapped the barrel to the left, knocking it offline with my heart. As it was, the gunshot exploded in the close confines of the cab, making me wince as the round tore out of the gun.

Fortunately, I've worked through loud bangs before. I know how to keep going while others get distracted. I ignored trying to twist the gun itself out of the cabbie's grasp. That would have been stupid. Instead, I went for the control of his hands and wrists. Gaining leverage there would ensure I had control of the gun. I'd seen enough badly taught gun disarms in my time to know that amateurs go after the gun.

Pros go after the limbs.

Cabbie let go of the gun with his right hand and tried to punch me with it. I used my left elbow to deflect the punch and leaned back, extending my legs and pulling his face into my shoes.

With his arm straightened out painfully, I twisted his wrist and heard the bone snap. Cabbie grunted and I could smell the odor on his breath - stale blood and over-cooked garlic. Neither a particularly pleasant scent on their own, the combination was even worse.

The gun came loose and I shot my left foot into the side of his neck. As he toppled back into the front seat, I righted myself and tore the car door open with my other hand.

The cabbie came out with one arm dangling useless at his side. He tried to throw a roundhouse kick at my temple, but I simply walked inside the arc of the kick and punched him in the throat with my free hand. He fell down on his ass, clutching at his larynx, coughing and retching.

I squatted next to him. I was already soaked with sweat.

Again.

"All right, sunshine. How about you answer a few questions this time." I placed my thumb under his nose and lifted his face up so he could see me. "Who tipped you off about me?"

"I was told you'd be at the airport waiting. That is all."

"Who do you work for?"

He shook his head. "If I tell you that, he will kill me."

I smiled. "No he won't."

"You don't know this man. He can kill you just by looking at you. His eyes, they are like the devil's. Able to kill with just a glance."

I frowned. What sort of bullshit was this? "How do I find this guy?"

"You want to find him?" He started laughing like I'd just suggested Santa Claus was going to hold a circle jerk for charity.

"Tell me."

"He will kill you, too."

"I've heard that before."

"He lives in Cabanatuam. North of Manila. He owns the city. They say he lives in a dark house where the light cannot find him."

"Paying his electric bill might help with that problem."

The cabbie shook his head. "He will know you are coming, Fixer. And he will wait until you are just about ready and then you will die."

"Speaking of which," I thumbed the hammer back on the gun. "It's about time for you to check out."

He started praying to someone. Didn't matter much to me. I shot him twice in the chest, the gun barking loudly in the blazing sun like an angry schnauzer. Two holes blossomed in his shirt, darkening the area with maroon blood.

He stayed defiant, though, cursing me out in Tagalog. His canines extended to their full length as he took his final breath.

I stayed with him another two minutes. Long enough to watch his teeth retract, ensuring that no one would ever know he was a vampire.

The shell casings gleamed in the bright sunlight and I plucked them off the ground. I dropped the magazine and checked the number of rounds still in it. I counted eight and then slid the mag back home. A quick jack of the slide to chamber a round and that was it.

I'd been in Manila a little over an hour and already I was laying the foundation for a bloodbath. People apparently knew I was coming – never a good thing in my line of work – and some evil overlord who lived in the dark didn't seem to like me very much.

I sighed and started walking toward where I hoped I could find a real taxi.

At least I had a gun now.

Something told me I'd be using it a helluva lot.

3
___

The Robinson Galleria housed a shopping mall on its lower levels and four-star rooms above it that actually featured air conditioning immune to the rolling brown-outs that affected most of the rest of metro Manila.

Did I mention it was hot?

I rode up the escalator to the main lobby on the second floor and asked for a room. The front desk clerk had a name tag that read 'Agamemnon," and against my normally sarcastic reflex, I ignored the obvious opportunity to have some fun with it, and opted instead to simply check in.

Upstairs, the elevator opened on a snoozing security guard positioned by the elevator banks on each floor to guard against possible Abu Sayaf kidnappings of guests. Looking at the grossly overweight sweaty slumbering ox in his chair with the 9mm Beretta snapped tight in its holster, I know I certainly felt better about my own safety.

Oh yeah.

I threw my bag on the bed and sat down. My shirt was stained from all the sweat I'd lost trekking over here after killing the cabbie and ditching his taxi. I saw myself in the mirror and decided that a shower would be the best thing to relieve my tired body.

I quickly glanced through the room service menu and phoned for lunch. Unfortunately, I also needed some juice. But somehow, I didn't think asking the room service attendant to give me a nip on his neck would do much for my preferred customer service status. I called Niles instead.

"I'm busy."

I looked at the clock. Two o'clock in the afternoon. That meant Niles was most likely in bed since it would be four in the morning back in Boston.

"I need some juice."

"So go bite someone. That's what I was in the midst of doing when I was so rudely interrupted."

I sighed. "Niles, I'm being serious."

"Dammit, so am I. You don't know how long it took me to land this guy, and I've finally got him right where I want him. Then you call."

"Do we have a network over here I can get a delivery from?" I was referring to the global network of blood banks most of my kind uses to keep themselves healthy. Not knowing what the vampire population of the Philippines was, I thought it might make sense to ask Niles.

He grumbled something into the phone and I heard him say something soft to the guy he'd shacked up with before closing the door. "If you ruin the mood here, I am never going to forgive you."

"I figure this makes us even for diverting my flight."

"Hmph." Niles must have turned his computer on because I heard him tapping some keys. "Are you near Cebu?"

"I'm in Manila, Niles. You know that. You put me in this godforsaken frying pan."

"In that case, no. There's no blood bank servicing that region."

"There are no Fixers over here?"

"Not in Manila, no. Now if you'll excuse me-"

"Niles. If I don't get some juice, I won't be able to complete your little errand."

He sighed and I heard more keys tapping. After another moment, he came back on the line. "All right. You're all set."

"What's that supposed to mean?"

"Good-bye, Lawson."

The phone clicked dead in my ear and I threw it on the bed. I made a mental note not to disturb Niles when he was busy seducing someone again. It affected his job performance, apparently.

I caught a whiff of something that smelled like dead cabbage and frowned. It was me. I shed my clothes and walked into the bathroom, turned the shower on and then placed the gun I'd taken from the cabbie on the back of the toilet before I stepped under the water.

The soap samples the hotel provided smelled like lavender, but I figured it was better than stinking like I'd just rolled around in a pile of used diapers. After lathering up three times, I rinsed and then turned the water to ice cold to snap my pores shut.

What should have been cold only came out as mildly cool. I frowned and shut the water off.

And stopped.

Water dribbled off of me, dripping to the shower floor while I stood there trying to make sense of the sudden change in air pressure in my room. Despite the fact I was in the bathroom, something felt weird.

Different.

Almost as if...

Shit.

Someone was in my room.

I moved slowly, reaching my hand out through the shower curtain towards the toilet, trying to get my hands on the pistol.

It was gone.

I looked out.

Nothing.

I bent and looked down on the floor just in case it had dropped. But there was no sign of the piece.

I grabbed at the towel closest to the shower and ran it over my head and then wrapped it around my waist. Whoever had come in to my room, they could have shot me while I showered, especially if they had grabbed the gun.

But they hadn't.

And I couldn't decide if that was good news or not.

My feet sank into the plush carpeting of the bath mat and I stood there for a minute, letting the undersides of my feet dry as much as possible. The breeze of cool air streaming out of the air conditioning vent made goose pimples break out all along my skin.

Everything, except for a few lingering drips from the faucets and the gentle hum of air conditioning, was silent.

I looked at the half open door and tried to figure out how best to play it. I could run through and scream my head off hoping to surprise whatever waited for me on the other side.

No way. If I was in that position, I'd be waiting with the gun aimed at where I'd approximate center mass.

Instead, I braced near the door jamb and sank low. Rater than peek around at normal height, I would try to get a glimpse down by knee level, hoping that whatever was out there wouldn't be quick enough to spot me and squeeze off a round.

I cursed the slumbering security guard. If he'd been awake

and alert, he might have seen this potential assassin come into my room.

I took a breath and risked the look.

Nothing.

I leaned back. Things still felt weird. There was tension in the air, but I couldn't find a source of it.

But the room was small enough that if I didn't see anything dangerous peeking around the corner, then perhaps I'd been mistaken. After all, I'd been on an airplane for the better part of a day. My brain was likely jumbled up.

I needed some juice and sleep.

I walked out of the bathroom.

Someone knocked on my door.

A quick glimpse through the peephole confirmed that my lunch had arrived. I certainly hoped the folks in the kitchen knew how to cook up a cheeseburger because I was starving.

I opened the door and let the room service guy in. He set up the table and placed the dishes on it, pointing out each thing by name. I saw him set out a few green packets.

"What are those?"

"Ketchup, sir."

I frowned. "What kind of ketchup is that?" I was used to the red variety, made from red things like tomatoes.

"Banana ketchup, sir. It's very good."

There are some things in life that simply do not go together. Like orange juice and toothpaste. Oral sex and people with rotting teeth.

Bananas and cheeseburgers?

"You have anything...tomato-based?"

He shook his head and held out his hand. I tipped him and then shut the door. How the hell do you even get ketchup from a banana?

"I don't much care for it, either."

I spun and found myself looking down the barrel of the gun I'd taken off the cabbie. For the second time in about two hours, I had a gun pointing at me.

Behind the gun was a beautiful Filipina woman. She had black hair that came down about shoulder length, dark almond eyes and light tan skin.

She looked at me in my towel, still wet with the water I hadn't wiped off my skin yet and shook her head.

"I don't know whether I should just shoot you, or screw your brains out."

I hoped she'd choose door number two.

4

"I suppose you've got a good reason for pointing that gun at me?"

She nodded. "The best reason of all: so you don't shoot me."

I couldn't argue with her logic. If I'd come out of the shower and known she was in the room, there was a fair chance she might have a round or two embedded in her. "And I shouldn't shoot you, is that it?"

"I'm here to help."

"Help?"

"Niles sent me."

I frowned. "Did he really?" I didn't move, but I kept watching for an opening when I could get a jump on her and take the gun away. I was cynical, obviously. These days, it didn't take much to eavesdrop on a cell phone conversation. Even though Fixer networks supposedly had some real good cutting-edge technology that prevented people from plucking our signals out of the air, I didn't believe it.

And I didn't believe her, either.

But the gun didn't move. She held it steady with both hands

and had her body formed into the a side-front position that would use her entire skeletal structure to properly absorb any recoil from the shots.

She'd been trained.

Well.

She watched my eyes travel over her, assessing. Tactically, she looked good.

Physically, she looked damned good, too.

But I couldn't let her looks distract me, as much fun as I might have doing so. I'm not crazy about beautiful women aiming guns at me, so even as I stood there seemingly not moving, I could feel my adrenaline streaming into my bloodstream and my heart hammering at my chest. Muscles started to ready themselves to spring forward as I started to count down.

I took a deep breath.

The intake of oxygen readied me even more. I subtly tried to flush myself with air, knowing my body would use it up when I took her down.

She showed no signs that she knew what was coming next. She only stood there still braced to fire.

I had to take the chance she couldn't squeeze the trigger fast enough.

Long odds to be sure, but I've faced worse. On three, I'd take her.

Three.

My thighs started to convulse as the adrenaline hit them.

Two.

I could taste a slight bitter flavor in my mouth.

One-

"*Hachvem eyol karang.*" The three words came out of her mouth and stopped me like a hard right from a heavyweight contender.

All the adrenaline bled out of my body like I'd just scored a bad case of the runs from a greasy spoon run by Chef Dave Dysentery. I almost wobbled as the tension slid away.

Instinct counts for a lot in my line of work. So does reflex. And what she said triggered an automatic response I'd rehearsed many times, but never used.

"*Saraq wutol anya.*"

She smiled and lowered the gun. "My name's Vikki. As I said, Niles sent me."

What she'd actually said was, "I serve the Balance." It was a recognition code in Taluk, the ancient vampire language and it identified her as a Loyalist – one of the very few humans who knew of the existence of my race. They'd pledged to help us long ago and it was something we depended on every once in a while.

But why Niles had sent her was anything but apparent. I held out my hand. "Do you mind?"

She glanced at the gun and then flipped it over and handed it to me. "Here you go. No hard feelings."

The butt of the pistol felt warm, but there was no sweat on it. Vikki was a cool customer. She'd have to be to face down a Fixer. And if I hadn't given her the proper code phrase back, which meant, "To you, our thanks," she would have shot me dead.

I put the gun down on the bureau and sat down in front of the room service cart and table. "You ever hear of banana ketchup?"

"It's gross."

I looked at her. She spoke with a vague accent. "You're from Manila?"

She sat down next to me on the bed. "I work in this hotel, actually."

She wasn't dressed like staff and I told her as much. She laughed and shook her head. "I own a jewelry store downstairs. It enables me to stay close without being obvious. And in the event nothing happens for years on end, I make a very nice living selling to Manila's high society and rich tourists."

"Plus, the annual salary you draw for being a Loyalist."

She smiled. "But that's stowed away in an offshore bank account until I serve forty years."

"True enough." I bit into the cheeseburger. It tasted a bit dry, but overall, it worked. I glanced at the banana ketchup and gave it a nanosecond of thought before opting to go without.

"You're not going to try it?"

"You said it was gross."

She smiled. "And you're taking my word for it?"

I put down the cheeseburger and wiped my mouth. "I thought we'd already established the whole trust thing when you had a gun aimed at me heart."

"I didn't think it would extend to the food, though."

I leaned back and looked her over. The gray pencil skirt she wore had light chalk lines running vertically down it. The white button down blouse and pearl necklace made her look like a classy corporate worker.

The ample view of her thighs the slit in her skirt showed off did not.

"Vikki, why exactly did Niles send you here today?"

"I got a call. Said you needed some help."

I reached for the glass of Pepsi and took a sip. "Did he tell you exactly what I needed help with?"

Her eyes twinkled. "Are we ever told beforehand?"

I shrugged. "Sometimes. And knowing Niles, yeah probably."

Vikki stood up and reached behind her waist. I heard the zipper come down and a second later the skirt fell, pooling around her ankles. She stepped out of it and stood in front of me in the blouse and pearls.

"He said you needed some juice."

I did. And considering that the sight of a woman in a blouse and very little else had always driven most of my blood into my crotch, I needed some pretty badly.

Vikki unbuttoned the first two buttons on her blouse. I could see the delicate white lace of her bra peek through, something that compounded the surge of blood under my towel.

I let my hands trace their way up the outside of her thighs, praying to every deity that this wouldn't be ruined by the appearance of boy shorts, only the worst and least appealing piece of lingerie ever invented.

My fingers found the thin band that meant she was wearing bikini panties.

There was a god.

Her breath tickled my ear as she lowered her head and kissed the side of my neck. "I'm all yours."

I decided to see if that was true.

5

Vikki lowered herself on to my lap and somehow managed to maneuver the towel away using only her thighs. I admire a woman who can work her hips as if she's using her hands.

"I've never been with a Fixer before."

"That makes two of us." I licked the side of her neck, tracing my way up toward her ear lobe and then back down.

Vikki's breath rustled my hair; her voice was a mere sigh. "Make love to me, Lawson."

She worked her way up and back until she had the connection she was looking for. I heard her suck a breath in as we joined and she leaned back to facilitate the process even further.

Her breasts seemed to strain against the fabric of her white blouse, threatening to burst through at any second. My fingers found the buttons and the material slackened each time I freed a restraint. I kissed her cleavage, feeling the warmth of her skin on either side of my face. Beneath my kisses, I could hear and feel the machine gun drum of her heartbeat crashing against her ribcage.

Vikki's lungs heaved, her inhalations coming in shorter more staccato gasps. She'd positioned herself at the most advantageous angle and judging by the wet heat down south, she was exactly where she wanted to be.

I waited until she was close and then grabbed her under her buttocks, tuned her over and positioned myself above her body, looking down into the never-ending abyss of her eyes.

She reached for me and brought our bodies together so that we became one single piston pulsing toward inevitable combustion.

"Lawson."

I kissed her hard on the lips, our tongues mashing together. She tasted sweet and the air around us was perfumed by the scent of our lust.

I drove harder.

Faster.

She moaned louder now and I could tell from the tiny muscle fluctuations cascading through her body that she was close. I could feel my own release building and I matched her rhythm to bring us over the edge at the same time.

At once her entire frame tightened.

Her breathing stopped.

I felt like she had me in a vise.

And then a single explosion of breath broke the silence of the room as we both tumbled slipped and toppled over the brink of orgasm.

I collapsed to the side of her, gulping down air. She rested her head on my chest and sighed, content in the afterglow. I let my hands wander through her hair.

"Sorry."

She glanced up at me. "What?"

I smiled. "I usually last much longer. When I haven't been on a plane for the better part of a day, I can go for hours."

She kissed my chest. "I don't have hours to spend in bed,

sweetheart. I do that and my business goes bankrupt. And that doesn't help either of us out much, now does it?

"Guess not."

"This was just fine."

I slid off the bed and grabbed another bite of my cheeseburger. It was cool now, but still edible. I offered some to Vikki. "Interested?"

"Not even remotely. I'm not a huge fan of the hotel's food."

I nodded. "Let me finish up my business in town and I'll take you out for Chinese."

"I know a place."

I smiled. "I'll bet you do."

She crawled over to me and rested her head on my shoulder. "This wasn't what I was sent here to do, you know."

"Yeah."

"Niles said you needed some juice. The sex was my way of saying welcome to the Philippines."

I looked at the way her hair fell on my shoulder and grinned. "If I could only get that kind of greeting in every country I have to visit, my life would be really grand."

Vikki reached over and took the steak knife from the room service cart. "How do you want to do it?" She mimed cutting her arm and I frowned.

"That's not exactly what I had in mind."

She leaned away and showed her neck. "More of a traditionalist are you?"

I shook my head and pointed at her right index finger. "You've got a bit of a hang nail there."

She glanced down. "I hadn't even noticed that."

"I smelled it."

She held her finger up. "Will it be enough?"

I examined her finger and looked at the small flap of skin

peeling back and away from her cuticle. "I might need to open it up some."

Vikki nodded. "Go ahead."

I leaned down and took the skin between my teeth. With a slight tug, I felt it give. Vikki gasped. A droplet of blood pooled along her cuticle bed and I sucked at it, feeling the warm coppery taste drip into my mouth.

I've never enjoyed drinking blood. It's not something that turns me on or makes me fell omnipotent. And I hate reading silly vampire stories where they romanticize the drinking of it.

But the fact was I needed it. My kind is able to take in blood and distill the life force energy from it, which in turn helps us live. The blood itself is simply a means of conveyance for the life force, nothing more.

Vikki's juice hit me almost instantly. I realized then that I'd been sorely lacking in energy. Hence my rather limited sexual ability.

I suckled her finger for another two minutes before coming up. The cardinal law in my society was never to take more than we needed and to leave no sign of our presence. So bite marks on the neck were silly. Besides, anyone who knows anything knows that biting through the thick muscle bands that ring the neck is dumb. There are far better places to take blood.

Vikki looked at me as I came up for air. "Feel better?"

I nodded. "Yeah. Thank you very much."

She leaned back and looked at her finger. My saliva had already clotted the wound. "Wow, already healed."

"It's a full service thing."

She unbuttoned the rest of her shirt. "Now that you're energized again, maybe you'd like to prove to me just how much staying power you really do have?"

"Thought you said you had to get back to work."

"Well," Vikki grinned. "There's something about seeing a naked man suck my finger that drives me crazy."

"Is that so?"

She nodded. "Yes, indeed."

Where she sat, the fading afternoon sunlight haloed her hair, making the strands furthest out look almost translucent. Her eyes crinkled as she smiled at me and I found the whole scene completely intoxicating.

The halo disappeared.

I frowned. A passing cloud-?

I heard the crash of glass-

-the harsh whisper plunging.

Vikki stiffened, her back arched back.

Her chest exploded bright red across my skin.

I dove for the floor, dragging her down with me.

"Lawson-"

The sunlight returned.

I looked at Vikki's chest. "Sniper. Probably on the roof across the way."

She grabbed my hand, but I could already feel the strength fading out of it. "I'm...sorry..."

I shook my head. "You did good."

"...brought them...to...you..."

"No. They knew about me already. Not your fault."

Tears rolled out of her eyes, staining her cheeks. I held her close, not caring about the blood on my skin.

She reached up for me. I bent low and kissed her. Her voice whispered one final thing.

"Get..them."

When I came up, she was dead.

I closed her eyes and hugged her one last time.

"I will."

6

Eight o'clock that evening found me sitting at a two-person table by the back wall of Szechuan Palace, the Chinese restaurant in the hotel. I had a black blazer on, far too heavy for a tropical environment, but with the air conditioning, things seemed tolerable enough. Where I should have had a pocket square, the clip of my Mont Blanc ballpoint pen showed enough to be a calling card.

Underneath the table, I had my bag ready to go. There was no way I'd be staying in the hotel tonight, not with Vikki's cooling body still upstairs in my room, along with the glass that had been shattered by the sniper bullet. Luckily for me, I'd brought along one bogus set of identification that I'd used when I'd checked in. The problem was I was a pale-faced foreigner. And even on the streets of Manila, it was enough to make people stop and stare at you. If my mug suddenly started showing up all over the evening news, I was going to have to exfiltrate this country through some backwater channel and delay my trip to Japan even more.

I wasn't crazy about that.

I had a Bombay Sapphire and tonic sitting in front of me. I'd squeezed the lime juice out of the wedge before letting it drop into the drink for color. And the taste of it brought me a certain sense of comfort. There are times when a good drink can do that – almost make you forget all the other shit going on in your life.

And there are times when a drink is like a magnet for even more shit.

Case in point: the dude who came into the restaurant, scanned it once and then headed for me like a horny virgin going for his first boob grab. I felt pretty certain that by the time this meeting was finished, my nipples were gong to hurt like he'd been trying to tune in Radio Free Europe.

By the way he walked, I could tell he was in a rush. Troubled, maybe. His stride was tight and fast. His eyes kept roving around like he suspected the whole thing was a set-up.

It was, but far be it for me to rain on his parade this early in the evening.

He slid into the chair opposite of me like he'd been expected. I gave him points for not standing in front of me and introducing himself. To anyone paying attention, we were tow chums meeting up for dinner.

"How ya doing?"

I took a sip of my drink wishing I was anywhere but there. "Been better. It's not important."

He held his hand across the table. "Name's Joey."

"Put your goddamned hand down. This isn't an AMWAY meeting."

Joey's hand vanished. "Sorry."

I leaned forward. "I don't care who you are. I don't care if you know who I am. What I am interested in is what you supposedly have for sale."

"Supposedly?"

I shrugged. "I haven't seen anything that would lead me to believe your claim is legit."

He leaned back. "It's legit. And it's worth a crapload of cash."

I took another sip and relished the taste of juniper berries mixed with lime. "Every salesman says that."

"You got a laptop?"

I shook my head. "Nope. But the hotel does out in the main lobby. We can check your merchandise there if you like."

"Yeah, cool." He pointed at my glass. "What's that you've got?"

"Bombay Sapphire, the world's finest freaking gin, and tonic water with a wedge of lime. Together they represent the pinnacle of an intoxicating evolution."

He frowned. "They got beer here?"

So much for my attempt to educate the great unwashed masses. "I imagine they've got something passing for that." I signaled the waiter over and Joey asked him for the list of brews. He settled on a San Miguel.

He would have been better off ordering yak piss.

I watched him guzzle the beer down and order another before he belched. Obviously, the guy was class.

"How'd you come by this merchandise?"

He set the second beer down on the table. "Got a guy who knows how to hack into anything. Couple of months ago he comes across a network he's never seen before. Got some crazy ass firewalls, high-level encryption, that kind of thing. I don't know much about it, I'm more into handling the sales."

"A people person, huh?"

He grinned. "That's me."

"So your friend-?"

"He hacks into the system. Took him the better part of a month to do it. But he manages to find a way in. What he sees amazes him. All sorts of stuff that don't make any sense. Names, numbers, all of it seemingly private and by that I'm talking like it wasn't related to any kind of government spook stuff, you know?"

"Yeah."

"So, now we've got this junk, but what to do with it? Not exactly the kind of thing you can advertise."

The lime in my drink was sinking toward the bottom of the glass. It looked lonely drifting in the clear mix. "But somehow you found a way."

"We put up a MySpace page."

I looked up at him. "You're kidding."

"Nah, the site's better than eBay for shit like this. Got ourselves a nice profile and started fielding friend requests, private messages, all that stuff. Before we knew it, we had a couple of interested parties."

I knew that the Council had recently implemented a computer security division that monitored the Internet for any signs that the Balance had been compromised. This was the first instance I'd heard of where it was panning out.

But something else disturbed me. "You said a couple of parties?"

Joey nodded. "Well, there's you obviously. And another dude here in the Philippines."

"Really."

Joey finished his beer and gestured for another. The waiter looked at me for a split second until I nodded. "Lives north of town. I told him I was meeting with you first and if it didn't work out, then he was next in line to see and bid on the merch."

I smiled. "Now why would you do a thing like that?"

Joey looked at me. "Huh?"

"You told another buyer about me. That's not very smart. In his place, I'd take steps to make sure I didn't factor into the equation."

"I don't understand."

"Of course you don't. You're a complete idiot. By telling the other party about me, you have made me a target. In fact, since I've been on the ground here, I've had two attempts on my life. I had no idea where they were coming from before you sat down, but now that you've told me about your vast idiocy, I know that this second party is behind both attempts."

Joey looked down at the table. "I thought I was-"

"Getting yourself positioned to make more money, yeah, sure I know how the greedy mindset works."

"Sorry 'bout that."

I finished the last of my drink and set the glass back down. "Let's go see what this merchandise of yours looks like. If it's good, we can deal. And then you can tell me all about this other interested party."

"Why would I do that?"

I smiled. "Because I need to make sure they don't stay interested."

7

Agamemnon was gracious enough to point us in the direction of the hotel computer bank situated by the front doors leading to the shopping mall. Joey and I sat down in faux leather chairs.

Joey reached into his jacket and produced a small translucent plastic fob about an inch wide and maybe twice as long. He plugged it into the USB port and I watched him click his way through the desktop folders until he found what he was looking for.

He glanced at me. "Ready?"

"Do it."

Instantly, the screen filled with a long list. I leaned in and examined the names. I recognized a few of them, but not all. That wasn't unusual. Fixer networks are structured so that we don't all know about each other.

But the names I did recognize left me with the distinct impression that Joey had the real deal plugged into the computer.

"All right. We can deal."

He eyed me. "So you saw something you know is true?"

"I said we can deal. Unplug that thing and erase any indication that it's been here."

He nodded. "All right." He unplugged the flash drive and I saw him stroke the keys until the data vanished. "All set."

We walked out of the computer room. Joey nodded to the front door. "You mind if we go outside for a sec? I need a smoke in the worst way."

"Those things'll kill you."

He laughed. "The circles I'm running in now with this stuff? I'll be lucky to see my 30th birthday."

The doors slid open and we walked through the shopping mall until we reached the end and exited to the outside. A balmy breeze sauntered through the evening sky. I didn't start to sweat immediately, which I considered progress.

Joey broke out his butts and lit one of them. I watched him suckle the butt and frowned. "So, why do what you do?"

He broke out laughing. "You kidding? The money's fantastic. Take this little puppy, for instance. Gotta be worth at least a couple million. Am I right?"

"Maybe."

He leveled a finger at me. "Don't play hardball now. I told you I've got another buyer lined up. You don't play fair, I'll take it to him."

"Where would that be anyway?"

"North. Place called Cabana something or other."

"Cabanatuam?"

He nodded. "You've heard of it?"

"Recently."

"I hear it's a dive, but hey, you go where the money is." He blew out another breath of smoke and I watched the breeze whip it away from us. Mercifully, I wouldn't be inhaling any of it tonight.

I looked out at the Manila skyline. The Makati section

housed the expensive shops and tall buildings peppered with neon signs and billboards written in what the locals called "Taglish," a mix of Tagalog and English. This was the ritzy part of town, removed from the trash heaps of the slums a few miles away.

"I'll give you a million five for it."

Joey smiled. "Two even."

"Done."

Joey stuck out his hand halfway until he saw me frowning again then he retracted it. "You don't shake hands much, do you?"

"No sense letting people know we just struck a deal."

"I guess not." Joey threw his cigarette to the ground. "You have the money?"

"In my room. You want to give me the flash drive now?"

Joey narrowed his eyes. "When I see the cash."

The promenade was empty but for the two of us. Now would be the time to do it. Joey hadn't given up the name of his hacker pal, but I didn't think there was much chance he would. We'd have to worry about him another time.

I reached behind my right hip where I position my pistol. Joey turned and looked out into the night. "This place isn't so bad, is it?"

My hand rested on the pistol grip. "A little hot for my taste."

He nodded. "Reminds me," he took out his cell phone and I froze.

"What are you doing?"

"Take a second," said Joey. "Gotta let the other buyer know we won't be dealing any time soon-"

"Joey-"

He held up his hand. I sighed.

Joey's voice was friendly enough as he talked to the guy on

the other end of the line. But I could see tension creep into his face.

"Hang up the phone, Joey."

He glanced at me, his voice already rising in anger with the person he spoke to. I drew my pistol and aimed it at him.

"Joey."

He saw the gun and froze in mid-speech. "I'll call you back."

I waved him over to the side of the concourse. "You shouldn't do that."

"I was just being courteous." He nodded at the gun. "What's that for?"

"You."

He chewed his lip. "We can forget the money."

"I already have. Now give me the flash drive."

Joey reached into his breast pocket and took it out. I gestured with the gun. "On the lip of the wall there, please."

Joey placed the drive on the wall. "Now what?"

"I need to know who hacked the system."

"You going to kill him, too?"

I shrugged. "Your friend wandered into something he shouldn't have seen. You brokered a deal that you never should have touched. This is how it ends, pal."

"I can forget everything."

"I can't take that risk."

"I won't tell you then. You won't get us both."

"Your choice. But I will find your friend eventually. I'm very good at what I do."

Joey held up his hands. "Make it quick, then because I-"

The shot came so quick and sudden I barely had time to register the tickle on my subconscious. As I watched, Joey's head simply exploded in a bright burst of pinkish red foam and gray bits of matter.

I threw myself on the ground as a second shot splanged off

the concrete nearest to me. The flash drive still sat on the lip of the wall. Judging by the shots, the sniper would have been on a roof opposite me. If I kept myself behind the wall, I'd be okay.

I eased closer to the wall. No doubt, the shooter would have his sights fixed on the flash drive, knowing I'd go for it. His finger would be on the trigger, ready to take the shot as soon as I presented my hand as a target. It wouldn't kill me, but it would make me pay heavy for trying to get the drive.

Joey's decapitated body had slumped to the ground. I yanked his corpse over, aware that he was wet with piss and feces already as his body's systems had started to shut down and the muscles relax.

I got his arm up and positioned it three feet from the drive. Then I got myself where I could grab the drive as soon as the sniper took his shot. I hoped he wasn't good at recalibrating himself quickly.

I poked Joey's arm up and a millisecond later as the bullet tore into Joey's arm, I swiped the flash drive from the wall and collapsed on the inside of it.

Safe.

I took a breath and fingered the drive. Such pain for such a small little thing.

"That was impressive."

I looked up. Two Filipino men stood about ten feet away from me. By the way one of them aimed the pistol at me, I could tell he was a pro.

"Get up, Lawson."

I nodded at the wall. "Someone on that roof doesn't like me very much."

"They won't fire while we're here."

"You're together?"

"Certainly."

I got to my feet, the flash drive in the palm of my hand. No way was I going to let them get it.

"I won't be naïve and ask you to lay your weapon down," said the second guy.

"Why not-?"

I felt a sudden hot lance shoot into my neck. Spots appeared in front of my eyes. Big black ones that grew in size.

Darkness rushed at me as the two men came closer.

"Good night, Lawson."

8

"Wake him up."

Through the impenetrable darkness, I heard the words and a second later felt the splash of cold water hit me. I tried to sit up but felt a steady pounding in my head. My mouth tasted like the backside of a camel.

"You're experiencing the after effects of a very powerful sedative. The best way to get over it is to simply get up."

I opened my eyes.

It was still dark.

Somewhere off in the darkness I thought I could hear a high-pitched whine, almost like the one you sometimes hear if the television is on. I thought I knew what it might be, but refrained from saying anything about it.

"You guys have any lights in here?"

"I prefer the darkness."

I had a sinking feeling I also knew whose presence I was in. The cabbie must have been telling the truth. I hoped his other information didn't turn out to be true.

"Why am I still alive?"

"You expected to be dead?"

I felt the wall behind my back and leaned into it. It felt a lot more solid than I did at that moment. "I tend to be problematic if my enemies keep me alive."

Laughter filled the air. "At least you're honest about it." I heard some movement, but nothing that made me suspect I was going to get the crap kicked out of me. Probably the sedative they'd shot me with had taken care of that.

"I have the flash drive, by the way. Just in case you were wondering."

"So I assume I'm in Cabantuam?"

"Correct."

I tried to let my eyes adjust. My race can see very well in the darkness, but something about this environment made it difficult to distinguish anything, even for me. "I'm still curious about being alive."

"Perhaps I wanted to talk to you."

"About what?" I needed to keep him talking. Information was my best advantage at this point. Trouble was, I didn't have much of it to work with.

"Everything in time, Lawson."

"You know me?"

"Of course."

"I'm not all that crazy about people knowing who I am and me not knowing who they are, you know? Kinda makes me a bit paranoid."

More laughter. "We knew you were coming."

"Your lackey said as much right before I killed him."

The voice paused. "So that's what became of him. We suspected as much but his body has not yet been recovered. We wondered what you did with him."

"Not a damned thing. I left him where I killed him: in some ghetto slums about a click and a half away from the hotel you shot me at."

"I appreciate your candor. We always prefer to have a proper burial and all."

I nodded. "No man left behind. I can dig it."

The high-pitched whine came from my left side. It was closer now. I glanced at the area using the corners of my eyes, letting the rods do their natural thing in the darkness. This time I could see the vague outline of a man, but not the one who was speaking.

Maybe security.

The high-pitched whine would have been his night vision goggles. I wasn't sure what kind of ambient light they were attempting to pick up in order to enable the guy to see better, but they must have worked somewhat.

It was a useful nugget of info I'd use later on. I cleared my throat, trying my best to get rid of the lump I had in it. Probably it was another wonderful leftover souvenir of the sedative. "So, any chance of you not looking at that flash drive?"

"None whatsoever."

"Pity."

"Would it surprise you to know that I've already looked at it?"

I frowned. "I guess not."

"I have. The information is quite fascinating. I'd heard rumors of how far and wide the Fixers were spread. I had no idea my race had its own global network of such accomplished operatives."

"Yeah, well, we like to keep a low profile. Helps us stay alive a little bit better than taking out a billboard ad in Times Square."

He chuckled. "I'm told you're a bit of a card."

"My reputation tends to precede me. Most of the bad guys I've dealt with tend to bring up my being a sarcastic prick."

"Indeed."

"Have you shown the information to anyone else?"

"Why would I? I wanted the information only for myself. It helps me in my business, you see."

"What business would that be?"

"Can't you tell? Drugs. The sedative we used on you is one of the ones we make especially for our race."

"I just got finished dealing with a similar operation in New York. You two aren't old school chums by any chance, are you?"

"No. But thank you for confirming what I'd heard. It means that New York is now a viable option for expansion. That is something I shall look into immediately."

I sighed. The taste in my mouth was slowly going away, helped in part by the trickle of water still dripping down my face. I licked at some of it, trying to hydrate myself as much as possible. It was the best way I knew how to help my system combat the drug.

"Glad I could help." The guy with the night vision goggles had moved closer. I estimated he was only about eight feet away. I could cover it in a heartbeat, but the trick was not letting him know I knew where he was. As it was, I'd have to guess and hope like hell he didn't have a gun aimed right at me when I made my move.

"The information that was on the flash drive is now safely stored at an offsite facility, just in case you think you'd like to destroy this place and me along with it."

"I was giving it some thought."

"But you don't really want to have to go through all that trouble, now do you? After all, I'd have to kill you. And I don't think you'd like that very much."

"This conversation isn't exactly blowing my skirt up. Would death be much worse?"

"What if I offered you a deal?"

"I don't deal."

"Yes, your integrity is legendary as well."

I frowned. "I don't know about integrity, but I can't be bribed."

"Even if the offer is too good to refuse?"

He'd stopped moving. The darkness grew still. I could hear breathing now. In front of me and on the left side of me.

"What's the deal?"

"I can give you the name of the human who hacked into your network."

9

"In exchange for what?"

If I could have seen the person behind the voice, I'm certain he would have shrugged. "Nothing much. Just that you leave me be with this information."

"I steer clear of you peddling drugs."

"Exactly."

"And the fact that you have access to Fixer networks."

"Consider it something like an insurance policy for me. This way, if you break your word, I'll have the option of going public with the information."

I frowned. "You'd sell out your own race?"

"In a heartbeat."

High-pitched whine hadn't changed his position. He must have been somewhere he felt confident in his ability to take me out if I tried something. I took a breath. "Tell me who the hacker is."

The voice paused. "I didn't think you'd agree to the proposition."

The guard to my left shifted. The energy in the room seemed to relax a bit as tension bled away. They would have likely killed me if I didn't bite at what they offered. "You can't always win every battle."

"And a wise man knows which ones he can't win."

I nodded. "Retires to fight another day."

"Wisdom."

"Hard gained, but wisdom nonetheless."

The voice chuckled. "I'd offer you a drink, but I have nothing here."

"I'll be happy with the name of the hacker."

"You'll kill him, of course."

"Of course."

"Which would mean I would be the only one aside from your Control and the Council who has this information."

"That's right."

"What would stop you from coming after me then? What assurance do I have that you won't?"

I sighed. "You just told me you had the information backed up at an offsite storage facility. I'd imagine you have some sort of fail safe as well. If you fail to check in the information is automatically released."

"Yes...yes, I do."

It sounded like bullshit to me. And because of his last question, I didn't think he did have the information backed up. In fact, I might have been unconscious for less time than I'd initially thought. It was possible that this guy had just the flash drive and little else.

Possible. But not definite.

"The name of the hacker, please."

"From your neck of the woods, Lawson. I believe he calls himself Benny the Phreak."

Shit.

I didn't say anything and in the next few seconds, the room filled with laughter. "You know him?"

"Yeah."

"How precious."

I gave him the moment. I tried to figure out what one of my valued contacts was doing selling me out. Not that Benny knew I was a vampire. But he knew that I was involved in the espionage world. I'd used him a couple of times in the past, most recently when I was working to protect a young vampire named Jack from a group of corrupt Council members.

I'd have to ask Benny myself what the hell was going on. But Benny was clear on the other side of the world.

And I was stuck in this dark pit of hell.

Which is why I chose that very moment – when the laughter was still echoing off the walls of the room – to lash out with a kick aimed at what I hoped might be chin level.

I connected and heard the grunt. A millisecond later, I heard the clatter of a gun.

A pair of arms tackled me as I scrambled for it. I've worked in the dark before and reliance on the rest of your body is paramount to coming out of it alive.

I shifted as a punch flew past my head. My attacker had night vision goggles on and could see me, but I knew they also distorted depth perception and would use that to my advantage if possible.

"Get him!"

I guessed the voice wasn't going to get involved. I had more immediate problems. The hands wrapped themselves around my neck, struggling to choke me out.

I clapped down hard on the top of his forearms using the side of my hands. The vital point on the top of the muscle aches when it gets hit.

The effect was instantaneous. The arms slackened and as they did, I shot another sword hand into the base of my attacker's throat. I heard him retch as his trachea collapsed under the assault. I hammered at him again, trying my best to fully collapse it and make breathing impossible.

He had forgotten about me now as he probably was clawing at his own throat, trying to relieve the pressure somehow.

I moved in and wrapped my left arm around the back of his head, jerked up and heard the snap I was looking for. The body in my arms went limp. As I let him slip from my grasp, his night vision goggles came off in my hand.

I slid them on and glanced around. The pistol was nearby and I scooped it up before looking at the rest of the room.

Bathed in the lime green luminescence, I could make out four walls, a desk, and one door leading out.

Seated behind the desk, was the man behind the voice.

He looked about forty-five years old in human years. Filipino with a balding head and a set of jowls tucked under his chin. The large wraparound sunglasses he wore made him look a bit like Jackie O. Just a far uglier version.

He hadn't moved since I'd killed his man.

That concerned me.

He must have known I was armed. But he gave no indication of being the slightest bit ruffled at the sudden power shift.

"You don't want this, Lawson."

I frowned. "You're not exactly in position to tell me what I do or don't want."

"You're still in my office."

"You need to call in a decorator. This place is appalling."

"I prefer Spartan."

"Not even a potted plant for crying out loud. It's bad Feng Shui you know."

He shifted but kept both his hands where I could see them. "That gun you're holding won't help you."

"No?"

"It isn't even loaded."

I hefted the piece. The weight felt right. "You sure about that? Feels like it's got some rounds in it."

"They're blanks."

I aimed the gun at him. No reaction. I squeezed the trigger, wincing as the explosion caromed around the walls and smacked my eardrums. A single shell spilled from the ejector and clinked onto the ground. I smelled cordite and gunpowder residue.

But the voice hadn't moved and showed no sign of injury.

"Put the gun down, Lawson."

"I'll hold on to it, thanks."

The voice sighed. "Very well. You leave me no other choice."

He reached to take off his sunglasses.

10

I whipped the gun sideways at him.
Something way back in the corner of my gray matter screamed at me when he started to take his glasses off. A vague memory helped propel my body into action and I watched the butt of the gun strike him right between his eyes, just above the bridge of his glasses.

The effect was instantaneous.

He reeled back, surprised, and then slumped to the floor unconscious.

I exhaled in a rush.

"That was close."

Hadn't the cabbie warned me that this guy could kill people just by looking at them? I was no mythology expert by any stretch of the imagination, but I wasn't keen on seeing if someone could Medusa me to death. No thanks.

I kept my head turned to the side as I made my way over to him. I felt his face to make sure the glasses were still on properly. They were. I checked his pulse and found it strong. He'd likely recover within a few minutes, although there'd be a nasty red welt where the gun had impacted.

His desk stood before me and I rummaged through the drawers, finding nothing but newspaper advertisements for girlie shows that touted amazing haircuts. It was a weird disconnect for me until I remembered that I'd been in other countries where a haircut meant something much different.

I stood back away from the desk. Why was there nothing inside but old newspapers? It didn't make sense. I felt around in my pockets but I'd been stripped of my wallet, phone, gun, and money.

Dammit.

One door led out of the office, but I wasn't crazy about going through it. For all I knew, there could be a dozen nasty dudes just waiting to beat the ever-loving ear wax out of me.

But Shades might be the kind of ticket I'd need to get through it intact.

A vague beep in the night vision gear made the decision for me. The batteries were dying. I got behind Shades and hefted him under his armpits. I took the gun as well – there might be some genuine ammunition outside.

All I had to do was find it.

Shades weighed a lot more than I would have guessed. It took far too much effort to get him upright and positioned close to the door. I juggled the gun and tried to work the door knob.

Locked.

There have been times in the past where I have played things as cautiously as possible. I've been on missions that have taken me so close to the edge of death that one tiny misstep would have spelled the end of my rather sorry albeit cynical existence. And generally speaking, I'm rather fond of taking my time.

You don't step on any landmines if you don't run.

However, there are just as many times when my patience runs a little thin. I'm not big on waiting. I never have been.

So, while the prudent thing would have been to set Shades down and try to somehow pick the lock, I was far too disgusted with the current state of affairs to do that. Instead, I leaned back, chambered my leg into my chest, and let a stomp kick hit the door just above the door knob, where experts tell you the door is weakest.

What I had failed to notice, however, were the hinges on my side of the door. So slamming my foot into the door jamb hurt like hell. And, of course, the door did not move one little bit.

After I'd cursed myself in a dozen languages, I took another second to examine the lock. This time I turned the door knob.

And pulled.

The door swung open leaving me feeling like very much the grand idiot.

I brought the gun up and swung out low, clearing left to right. Even though the gun didn't have real bullets, the appearance might buy me some time in case there were bad guys out there.

The door opened on to a hallway.

Empty.

I ducked back inside the office and got my arms under Shades' armpits and dragged him outside. The light in the hallway wasn't much better, but I could at least see even without the night vision goggles on.

I pulled Shades out into the hallway. I had two options and chose right. At the end of the hallway, I could see another door and aimed for that.

Unfortunately, I also had to decide to either drag Shades along for the ride or leave him be. Dragging him along meant I'd have to turn my back as I maneuvered up the corridor. Not the best position to be in tactically.

But if I left him behind, I'd be giving up any bargaining power I thought his presence might afford me.

There was another option but I wasn't crazy about it.

I set Shades down and then bent him over my shoulders in the modified fireman's carry position. At least this way I could see where I was going and hopefully get there in one piece.

I kept the pistol up with my right and held onto Shades with my left.

As I moved, I thought I could hear voices ahead of me. They were speaking Tagalog, one of the few languages I don't actually speak all that well.

I heard laughter.

I got up close to the door and leaned against the wall trying to catch my breath. Shades was proving heavier than I'd expected. And I was also working on not much energy.

I thought about Vikki for a moment and saw her face again in my mind. She'd given her life for my race,, something she hadn't been obligated to do. I respected her immensely for that, and I'd make sure she hadn't died in vain. It seemed like lately, I'd been doing that far too often.

I really needed to get to Japan.

I took a moment by the door to take a breath and compose myself. I held the gun down and at the ready, dearly hoping its appearance would be enough to take advantage of everyone in the room for the moment I needed.

It was time.

I braced outside the door, this time checking to make sure it opened inward before I jammed my other leg.

It did.

I took another breath, balanced Shades on my shoulders, and then unleashed the kick.

The door shattered.

As I breached the room, I immediately counted four men, all armed.

My gun came up.

"Don't even think about it."

I had the hammer back – visible so they could see I wasn't playing.

Instead of the shocked expression I'd been hoping, the only thing that greeted me was more laughter.

And that didn't make me feel good.

Not one little bit.

11

"He looks heavy."

I let Shades slide off of my shoulders and slump to the floor. I kept the gun aimed at the four guys as much as I could, but they seemed unfazed by it. One of them actually pointed at it.

"He thinks we don't know."

I frowned. "Don't know what?"

"About the blanks," said another one.

None of them had reached for their own weapons yet. I sidled a little bit closer to where I'd dumped Shades. Maybe I could rip his glasses off and turn them all to stone or whatever it was this dude was supposed to be able to do to people.

They just stared at me with bemused looks. I really hate that kind of smugness. Behind them I saw a bank of television monitors. "What are those for?"

One of the guys pulled out a chair from a nearby table and sat down. He slapped his feet up on to the table and leaned back. "Don't you know? We've been watching you for the past half hour."

"Surveillance?"

He nodded. "Impressive the way you took care of Buchoi like that."

"What kind of name is that?"

"Not really a name. But we like to call him 'Fat Boy.'" He smirked. "We Filipinos tend to be rather blunt in our personal estimations."

"So, you've known-"

"-that you were headed this way. Yes."

"And the laughter?"

"The way you struggled with the door for one."

I felt my face go red. "It was dark."

He pointed at my head. "You did have the night vision goggles on. But then again, I suppose it might have been too much to expect that you'd check something so elementary like that."

"Yeah, well, everyone makes mistakes." I saw a door down toward the back of the room. The hinges were on this side.

"We also enjoyed watching you struggle to haul Eric up here."

"Eric?"

He pointed at the slumped form of Shades. "Him."

"I thought he was-"

"-the boss?" He laughed. "Not even close. But he does make for a real nifty impersonator if we need him to."

I sighed. "Let me guess: this whole thing is a sham. There is no guy here who can kill you just by looking at you."

The guy shrugged. "What can we say, we enjoy a good myth as much as the next crime family. And it's certainly helped us spread the fear. People don't mess with us all that much. The rumors and all help keep people very nicely in their proper places."

"Nice trick." I glanced at Shades who was starting to groan

on the floor. I felt like caving his skull in with the heel of my foot.

The guy at the table examined his fingernails, found something he liked, and proceeded to pick at it until I caught the scent of blood on the air. He smiled and saw my sudden attention.

"You looking for this?" he held up his finger. I could see the crimson line dribbling down his finger. My mouth went wet with saliva. A little juice would go a long way to restoring my energy levels and help me finish these assholes off.

"No."

He laughed. "Liar." He sucked the blood off of his own finger. "Wouldn't do you any good, anyway. We're just like you, Lawson. Members of your very own race and we all know that you won't get much of anything from our own blood."

He was right. Drinking a vampire's blood would only grant the tiniest fraction of energy to another vampire.

"I wasn't aware the vampire population in the Philippines was quite so large."

He shrugged. "It's not. Probably under a hundred in total. But we control a lot of the underside of society here. Gun running, drugs, prostitution, gambling. We moved into power when the country finally got rid of the Marcos clan. We've been doing it ever since."

"Always nice to hear about these success stories," I said. "Really warms my heart to know vampires are out there making it big by causing strife in the world, dude."

"Call me Jorell."

"Like Superman's father?" I shook my head. "What do you guys use for baby names over here? The Iliad and comic books?"

Jorell frowned. "I happen to like my name."

"Well, sure, who wouldn't? By the way, you can call me Logan."

"I thought your name was Lawson."

I sighed. "Never mind, genius. It's an apparently obscure reference. Either that or you don't get Marvel over here."

Jorell let it go, which was probably just as well. He pointed at me. "You've got yourself a bit of a big problem. Haven't you?"

"Not really?"

His eyes widened. "No?"

"Way I see it, I have a bunch of people who need to be killed here. The only question I have is which one I kill first."

Jorell chuckled. And then he laughed. Behind him, his lug nut henchmen joined in and together they produced a discordant chorus of idiocy. I've heard coyotes that had more natural talent.

"First one to kill." Jorell wiped his eyes. "You are a funny man, Lawson. We knew that when we decided that it was time to kill you before you became a thorn in our side."

"Now, why on earth would you want to kill me? My theater of operations is the Northeast of the United States. I usually work out of Boston. Not Manila."

Jorell smiled. "But you are also the Fixer the Council turns to when they know other Fixers can't handle the pressure of the task at hand. You are their go-to fellow. The one they unleash when things are really bad."

"It's not even close to being as awesome as you make it sound."

Jorell ignored me. "We like to plan ahead. And we recognized that our own success would invariably draw the Council's wrath. At that point, they would have little choice but to unleash their prized killer on to us. One way or another, you would end up here in the Philippines with a mission to dismantle what we've worked so hard to establish."

I shrugged. "If you say so."

"We do. And more importantly, she does, too."

"She?"

Jorell grinned. "In good time. Right now, we thought it might be nice if you saw an old friend of yours." He snapped his fingers and the door behind him opened up.

I saw him but didn't believe it until he pushed his way through the thugs and grinned at me.

"Hello, Lawson."

He looked like he'd cleaned up a lot more than the last time I'd seen him. But he still had a lot of weight to lose and his hair was still a greasy mess of crap. He wore a garish Hawaiian shirt and baggy shorts.

"Hi Benny."

12

"You look surprised."

I shrugged. "Halfway around the damned world and you show up out of the blue shortly after I learn you've betrayed me. Yeah, I guess you could color me a little shocked and awed."

Benny shook his head. "Now, now, I didn't actually betray you. That's a bit of an overstatement. I never knew what you were. Just that you were...something."

"Your ignorance is a convenient excuse. I've killed men less stupid than that and not even given it a second thought."

"When I stumbled upon the network, I knew I had something special. I just never dreamed what I had was this special."

I nodded at Jorell. "And you think these guys are going to let you live?"

"Why not? I've given them what they wanted most: you."

It wasn't about the network at all. "This was to get me?"

Jorell looked like he was enjoying himself far too much. "You are rather slow sometimes, Lawson. Has anyone ever told you that?"

"It's been mentioned."

"When Benny made inquiries about what he'd found, we realized we had a golden opportunity. In one move we could get our hands on not only the Fixer networks, but also the Council's most prized Fixer himself."

"That'd be you," said Benny.

"We covered that already," I said. "I'm a little beyond the whole flattery thing."

Jorell smiled. "We approached Benny and he agreed that selling us the information was most beneficial for his future plans."

I looked at Benny. "Future plans?"

He shrugged. "I'm getting married."

"She know how you're funding the reception?"

"She could care less about what I do, as long as the money's there." Benny sighed. "She's a materialist."

"Swell." I looked Benny in the eye. Hard. "And just when did they tell you that getting me was the goal?"

Benny turned away. "We were never friends, Lawson."

"My mistake," I said. "Thinking that all the times we did business and that one time I helped you out of a jam would count for a little something beyond the green."

"Yeah, well, I repaid that debt. It's history."

"There was no debt, you asshat. I never thought you owed me a thing. Helping you was something I just did. Just because. You understand that?"

He stared at me like I'd suggested that computers were only a fad.

Jorell cleared his throat. "I think the important thing to remember here is that while yes, Benny did indeed sell you out and stab you in the back rather viciously, what matters most is that you are here now. Right where we wanted you to be."

"And I'm thrilled about that, believe me."

Benny drifted back to the corner of the room.

I leveled a finger on him. "Don't even think about going anywhere. You and I aren't through."

He shrugged. "I think you might be, though."

Jorell chuckled. "He's right."

I kept my hands loose by my sides. "So, you've got me. Now what happens? You going to kill me or what?"

"We already offered you a deal."

I nudged Eric's slumped form. He was struggling to roust himself. I gave him a solid kick for good measure and he slumped over again. "You mean this clown?"

"Don't kick him again. We might need him alive for some reason."

I whistled. "Company loyalty here amazes me. You guys have benefits, too?"

"You turned the offer down. Remember?"

"Forget about that. Make me a new offer."

Jorell's smile faded. "Are you serious?"

I grinned. "I'm always looking out for number one. That's what I told that idiot."

"We thought you were just telling him that to buy time."

"Maybe. Try me out and see how it goes down."

Jorell leaned back. "All right. You work for us. You do exactly what you do right now: kill other vampires."

"I kill humans, too. On occasion."

Jorell nodded. "I forgot."

I glanced at Benny. "I hope you weren't too attached to Joey."

Benny's eyes widened. "You killed Joey?"

"Well, not me. These guys here. Took his head apart with a sniper rifle. By the way it exploded, I'd guess a 7.62, but then again, a good head shot can explode the gray matter like a ripe watermelon."

Benny came over to Jorell. "You told me Lawson killed him."

I smirked. "Oh, I was planning to. Don't get me wrong. It's just your new pals here beat me to the punch, so to speak."

"I told you he had to be left alive. He's my fiancé's brother, for fuck's sake."

I shook my head. "Uh oh, looks like there might be some trouble in paradise, pal. She's not going to like finding out her brother needs a closed casket."

Jorell turned to Benny. "if there had been a way to keep him alive, we would have."

I nodded. "Sure. I believe that."

Benny sighed. "I am so screwed."

Jorell pushed him away and turned back to me. "That wasn't necessary."

I held up my hands. "Hey, I was just being honest."

"And like I said, unnecessary."

"Can't help it. I've got this troublesome integrity thing going on."

Jorell ignored me. "All right. You will continue to do what you do best, Lawson."

"Be a funny guy?"

"Kill."

"Okay."

"In exchange, we won't kill you. But you'll do whatever we ask you to do. No questions asked. Your assignments will generally help us pave the way for our future success. You'll remove troublesome characters standing in the way of our progression."

"I could handle that."

"You're actually interested?"

I shrugged. "Sounds better than dying."

Benny came back to life. "You can't be serious."

Jorell glanced at him. "You're annoying me."

I smirked. "Tell you what, Jorell."

He looked back at me. "What?"

"I'll take the job. But I want one thing in return."

"What's that?"

I pointed at Benny. "Him."

13

"You're out of your mind, Lawson."

I glanced at Benny. "Am I?" My gaze moved to Jorell who had placed his index finger in his mouth and seemed lost of thought.

Benny followed my eyes and when he saw that Jorell hadn't dismissed the idea as ludicrous immediately after I'd proposed it, his expression changed from one of confidence to one of uncertainty.

Time to press the attack. "It's not open to negotiation."

Jorell looked up at me. "You'll kill him?"

"Yes."

Benny turned to me. "Lawson, we go way back, man. All those times together, the information I've given you-"

"-charged me for, Benny. I had a helluva time with my expense reports because of you and your high prices."

"Even still."

"Even still you were a valuable asset. Able to deliver the goods when I needed them. I never expected that you would try to betray all the trust we'd built up. If there's one thing that sickens me like nothing else, it's a traitor."

His head slumped forward. "It was the money."

"You had plenty of it before. Why would you even need to get in bed with these people?"

"It's gone."

"What is?"

"The money. All of it. I gambled it away on the Internet."

I shook my head. "That doesn't make any sense. You never paid a bill in your life once you figured out how to break into computer networks and change the decimal points."

"I couldn't keep up with the improvements in network security. And one day, it was all gone. My credit cards were maxed out. I had foreclosures on my properties. I had to sell it all."

"And you're still getting married?"

He shrugged. "I think she loves me for me, if you can believe that."

I smirked. "It's a lot to swallow, Benny. And the simple truth is you were more than ready to see these guys kill me. Why should I give you any quarter when you would have given me none?"

"Because of our past, dude. What we had was something special. We worked well together. Especially on that double-agent case. You remember?"

I frowned. "The false flag thing, right?"

"Yeah."

I sighed. "We had some good time, Benny. But you went bad on me. And if I let you go, it sets a bad precedent. I don't give my enemies any wiggle room. And you are no exception."

Jorell stood. "He's yours."

Benny's eyes went wide. "You can't be serious! I brought him to you. I gave you all the information you wanted. Did everything you asked of me. You can't do this!"

Jorell looked him over. "We would have killed you anyway. The truth is, you're quite annoying. And since we now have exactly what we wanted, you have become well, rather expendable. The ability to bring Lawson in to our little family is far more attractive than keeping you around. No offense, of course."

Benny slumped back against the wall, mumbling to himself. I watched the color drain out of his face as I held out my hand to Jorell. "We square?"

He nodded. "Your word on this?"

I grasped his hand and shook it. "You've got it."

Jorell nodded at Benny. "You want to kill him now or later?"

"Now is as good a time as any."

"All right. Don't mind us if we watch." He leaned in closer to me. "After you kill him, you might as well have a quick drink. A little blood for your trouble, so to speak."

"Yeah, I don't think so." I turned away. "Truth is, he's a bit negligent on the whole body hygiene thing. I'm not all that crazy about the idea of sampling some of his juice if you follow me."

"I understand." Jorell turned to one of his henchmen and said something quickly. The guy disappeared out the back door and returned a moment later carrying a flask. He gave it to Jorell who in turn handed it to me. "You want some of our own brew?"

I took the flask and tilted it back to my lips. It was mercifully chilled to the right temperature and I drank deep. It was fresh and the jolt of energy it gave me surged through my system almost making me break out in a sweat.

I gave the flask back. "Thanks."

Jorell smiled. "How do you want to kill him?"

"A gun's fine."

"You're not going to do it with your bare hands?"

I smiled. "What-you guys want a show?"

Jorell shrugged. "I figured you might be annoyed enough with his betrayal to want to tear his head off."

"Oh, I am. But I also don't like getting a mess on my clothes.

And since I'm already a bit gamey and in need of a shower, I don't see how adding to that will be a good thing."

Jorell nodded. "All right." He reached behind him and pulled out a small Walther .380 pistol. "You're sure he's not one of us, right?"

"Yeah, why?"

Jorell hefted the gun. "This has regular bullets in it. Only good for humans. After all, we don't want you walking around with those vampire rounds now do we?"

I chuckled. "And here I thought we had all of this trust now that I'm working for you."

"Call it careful cautiousness if you like."

I took the gun from him. "Doesn't matter. Once I take care of Benny, I think we'll be a lot closer to where we need to be in terms of trust."

Jorell smiled. "I agree most wholeheartedly."

Benny cowered against the back wall, shifting and mumbling still. I cold see the sweat stain marring the plaster, giving it the appearance of a slug that has just left a goo trail in his wake.

"It's been fun, Benny."

He looked up at me. "Lawson..."

"I brought the gun up and sighted down the barrel, lining up the sight picture until it was exactly where I wanted it.

I eased the hammer back.

Benny whimpered.

I fired.

14

The bullet slammed into Benny and spun him around and down into the floor. He lay there crumpled like a used napkin smeared with cheap red lipstick.

I watched him for a second and then looked back at Jorell. "Thanks."

Jorell smiled. "My pleasure. To be honest, I wasn't sure you'd do it."

"Why not?"

He shrugged. "You had a history with him. I thought that relationship might count for something."

I handed him the gun. "Loyalty counts for more than any number of years spent lining someone's pockets with money. Benny chose to hire himself out to the highest bidder and fucked me over in the process. By doing so, he put himself on the endangered species list."

"Apparently."

I nodded back at the body. "You'll dispose of the body?"

"Sure. We'll use him for bait when we fish for tiger sharks off of Cebu. They grow pretty big down there. I'm sure a little Benny will do wonders to draw in the bog boys."

"No doubt." I sat down at the table. "So, what happens now?"

Jorell sat across from me. Behind him, the henchmen vacated the room without being told. I appreciated the way Jorell had non verbal control over his men. We waited until the door closed and then Jorell spread his hands on the table.

"Are you ready for your first job?"

I frowned. "You've got a target for me already?"

"Certainly."

"But we only just came to an agreement."

"Well, maybe not."

I frowned. "What the hell does that mean?"

Jorell leaned back. "We've had our eyes on you for a long time, Lawson. Ever since you first showed up on the radar screen we knew it would behoove us to find a way to get you over to our side."

"And when did I first show up on your screen?"

"A few years ago. You did a job in Singapore. Do you remember it?"

"I remember all of my jobs. Some of them with a lot less fondness than others, but they're all stored in my head. I'm told there are lessons in there I should learn from. Not sure if I believe that or not, but what the hell."

"We had some business interests in Singapore at the time. Of course, we were far less organized than we are now. Your sudden appearance at the airport that night made for some rather complicated choreography, so to speak."

It had been a shipment of machine guns bound for some fourth-world dictator who'd been oppressing people for years. The sheer number of bodies he'd stacked like lumber had been deemed a threat to vampire security. We'd already gotten word that he had slaughtered several of our people in the midst of normal humans. While the Council dispatched a STA-F team to take care of his cabinet and eventually the dictator himself, I'd been sent to put an end to the people supplying him with weapons.

I'd followed the trail from a Chinese mercantile company that had routed the weapons through Taiwan and then into Singapore where they were supposed to get slotted into a cargo jet bound for the tropical slaughterhouse.

That never happened. At the same time the Special Tactics Assault-Fixer team was working their way through the imperial palace two thousand miles to the west, I was double-tapping the arms smugglers and planting enough high explosive to send a clear message to whoever was behind the weapons shipments that they would not be tolerated any longer.

"I didn't think I left anyone alive," I said. "I usually take precautions the ensure that doesn't happen."

"We arrived late. Probably just after you left." Jorell smiled. "You made quite a statement with the fireball engulfing the plane."

"I was told to."

"And you follow orders."

"Mostly." I smirked. "I've had my share of ones I don't do well with."

"As well as sending a message to the people behind the shipment, you also made quite the impression. I took us almost a year to dig up enough information on you to prepare a dossier."

"You've got a dossier on me?"

"Any recruitment attempt is always preceded by exhaustive research. Surely you understand that better than most."

I leaned back in my chair and looked at him. "Yeah. I know it. Doesn't mean I like knowing there's a packet of papers on me detailing my life. You might have gotten a few things wrong in the process."

Jorell shrugged. "It's possible. But we were pretty careful."

"Maybe you should let me see it. Just to make sure."

He grinned. "I don't think that's necessary any longer. After all, we've got a deal with you now."

"And a target apparently."

"Yes."

I leaned forward. "Here or elsewhere?"

"Back in Boston."

I frowned. "Who is it?"

"Your Control. Niles."

I smirked. "Why on earth would you want him killed?"

"That's on a need-to-know. Yours is no longer to question why, it's simply to follow our orders."

I took a breath. "You know what this whole thing sounds like?"

"What?"

"A massive set-up."

Jorell frowned. "I'm not sure I know-"

"-yeah. You do." My head hurt but I was pretty sure of what was going on here. "You did your research on me and discovered what I was and that it might be cool to actually get a genuine Fixer working for you. So you took steps to manufacture a situation where that could happen."

Jorell didn't say a word so I kept going.

"And when Benny there started fishing around for prospects on his information, you moved in. But you didn't care about the network information he had, did you? All you cared about was offering him up to me in exchange for my loyalty."

Jorell stared at me and then the briefest glimpse of a smile parted his lips. He glanced at the ceiling and raised his voice.

"You want to do this or should I?"

The door behind him opened.

A tall woman I'd never seen before walked in. She wore sunglasses and her hair draped about her head in long tightly coiled braids. She smiled at me but there was nothing friendly about it. The aura that surrounded her emanated nothing but evil.

She laid a hand on Jorell's shoulder. "You've done well."

"He's very astute."

"We knew this before we started."

I frowned. "Hello? I'm still sitting here."

She turned and looked at me. "Hello, Lawson. I think it's about time we got better acquainted."

I waited for her to take off the glasses, but she didn't.

Instead, she leaned closer and hissed. "Call me Miranda."

15

The blackened lenses gave her a distinctly buggish look. But the tightly coiled braids of her hair made her resemble something that might have come out of a special effects workshop in Hollywood. Judging by how her nose and lips formed a certain geometric shape, I could tell she might be almost eerily beautiful. But since I'm a sucker for a good set of alluring eyes, I couldn't pronounce her certifiably hot.

Probably better for me since I really had to concentrate on the business of getting my job done.

She regarded me for another moment like she was searching for something. Maybe she was trying to read my thoughts. She wouldn't get much. I'd spent years learning how to empty my mind of anything remotely intellectual by subscribing to vacuous entertainment magazines big on pictures and short on much else.

"So this is him."

She leaned back against the table. I saw she was wearing a long flowing dress decorated with some bizarre pattern of blacks, golds, browns, and deep crimson. The effect was vaguely unbalancing.

I pointed at the dress. "If I stare at that long enough, will I see a rocket ship heading to moon?"

The smile that parted her lips revealed a set of too-white teeth. "You might just see your future in it."

"How's that?"

"The dress reveals many things. It's just a question of what you want to see." She folded her arms, making her breasts come together and deepening the cleavage. "What do you want to see, Lawson?"

I smirked. "Is this a trick question?"

"Jorell tells me you that are the best at what you do – that you are the Council's top man in the field. A Fixer among Fixers. Is this true?"

I shrugged. "I don't toot my own horn. It's a bit gauche."

"Jorell tells me that your capacity for dealing death is also unrivaled among your peers."

"There's more to my job than just killing."

She nodded. "I've read your files. I know of some of your assignments. Saving the little boy was a bit out of your normal realm, wasn't it?"

"Yes."

"But you succeeded marvelously. Almost as if you have the ability to blend in with whatever is necessary to get the job done."

"I was trained to be that way."

She waved her hands. "Please. The Council trains its Fixers to be little more than glorified killers."

"You're confusing that with other units within the service."

She leaned forward a bit, quieting her voice. "You mean like the Specters?"

I cleared my throat. "Yeah. Like them."

"But the Council calls them a security force. Specialized camouflage and infiltration tactics make them the ideals for protecting the Council's favorite little hideaways, like the Invoker school your friend Jack attends."

She stood and walked around the table. "The reality is the Specter units are almost entirely without conscience. They are designed to be last-ditch solutions to human encroachment on vampire strongholds."

"If this is leading somewhere, I'd really appreciate you getting to the point. I apparently have a plane to catch to Boston by way of Japan."

Miranda glanced at Jorell. "Japan?"

Jorell shrugged. "He was on his way there when he was diverted here into our waiting arms."

She looked back at me. "And what, pray tell, is in Japan."

"My sanity, near as I can figure it."

"Are you losing your marbles, Lawson?"

"Burnout," I said. "My last few jobs have gone bad. Not so far as to say failure, but there have been too many collateral casualties. I've lost friends. And innocents as well who had business being in the cross-fire."

"And you feel responsible."

"Of course."

She smiled. Something about her teeth seemed too perfect. I worry when people have choppers that look like they were popped out of a mold an hour before and slid into place.

"I like your sense of responsibility."

"Don't tell my mom, she'll get all weepy proud."

"Your mother is dead." Miranda's smile never wavered. "Or didn't you know we knew all about that as well?"

"Know about what?"

"The facts surrounding the death of your mother. It's something you've always wanted to know, isn't it?"

"My mother died in a car crash."

"You're still trying to sell yourself on that one?" Miranda nodded. "I suppose you'd have to, wouldn't you? Given the nature of your job, the idea that someone manufactured her demise might well upset you enough to go and administer a little bit of justice."

"I'm not into conspiracy theories."

Miranda nodded. "Tell me something: how did you reconcile the notion that you weren't at her funeral because you were in the Fixer Academy at the time? Surely,, you could have gotten leave to attend."

I sucked at my lip. No way did I like where this was heading. "We were on an FTX – a field training exercise – at the time. Leaving wasn't an option."

"Not even for your mother?"

I stood up. "You know about me? You think you know all about what I stand for and what goes on in my head just because someone fed you some classified documents? You've got no idea. When the Council told me what I was destined to become, I wanted no part of it. It was only later that I grew to respect the ideals."

Miranda sighed. "Before all, the Balance."

"Damn straight."

She glanced at Jorell. "And you really think that you've broken him? You really and truly believe that we now have control of this Fixer?"

Jorell stammered. "Sure, I mean, why wouldn't I? He just killed one of his oldest contacts. Right in front of me."

Miranda sighed again and this time she closed her eyes. Her head tilted back and I saw the tip of her tongue snake out past her lips, almost as if she was tasting the air. It flicked back in and out a few more times.

"Fool." Miranda's voice was almost a whisper.

Jorell shook his head. "What-?"

Miranda pointed at Benny's corpse. "He's not dead at all. You idiot!"

16

Benny lurched and rolled over so he faced us. As he did so, his right hand unfurled and I saw the pistol come flying toward me.

"Lawson!"

I grabbed it, felt the warmth in my palm as I flicked the hammer back and aimed it at Miranda and Jorell. "Don't either of you move."

Benny struggled to his feet behind me and came up. "Nice shot."

"You hurt bad?"

He shook his head. "Niles told me you had good aim, but I never would have believed it unless you shot me."

"So now you're a believer."

He smirked. "Guess so. A bloody one, but yeah."

"Is the bullet still in there?"

Benny poked at his shoulder and flinched. "Feels like it. The bleeding seems to have stopped though."

"We finish this, we'll get you to a doctor and get it patched up. You'll be back cracking codes in no time."

"I'm just glad you understood the message."

I nodded. "You were pretty convincing. And I was pretty close to actually killing you until you mentioned the code phrase."

"I was so nervous, I almost forgot."

Miranda hadn't moved, almost as if she was content to watch this reunion play out. That made me nervous. Next to her, Jorell didn't look so good.

"You okay Jorell?"

Miranda snickered. "Not for much longer."

"What the hell does that mean?"

She smiled, showing those white teeth again. And then she turned her head to look at Jorell.

He screamed. "No!"

Miranda removed her sunglasses. Instantly, Jorell's skin started to peel back away from his skull. Flaps of it tore away from the tendons underneath. Capillaries burst. Jorell's eyes grew wider and wider as more of the orb exposed itself.

He clutched at his throat, a plaintive shriek bubbling up from somewhere deep in the haunted reaches of his soul.

Blood poured out of his mouth now, mixing with the crimson flow from what used to be his face. His entire head seemed to be melting into one putrid mass of melted flesh.

Next to me, Benny vomited.

Miranda started laughing now as Jorell sank to his knees. I saw one of his eyeballs pop out of his skull, dangling by the optic nerve the way they sometimes showed it in the cartoons.

She kept laughing as Jorell toppled over to one side, the gooey flow of blood and liquefied flesh streaming over the floor to where Miranda's feet were. Jorell's final shriek was more of a gasping belch before he twitched one final time and then lay mercifully still.

Miranda knelt down and dipped her finger into the fleshy

fondue that had been Jorell's head, brought it to her lips, and then suckled it for a moment.

Benny puked again.

"Delicious," said Miranda as she slid her glasses back on as she stood back up. "I always knew he'd be worth waiting for."

I kept the gun steady even though my own stomach was tumbling. I handle cannibalism about as well as I handle seeing autopsies.

Which is to say, not well at freaking all.

"You make any move to take those glasses off and I will shoot you very fucking dead."

She smiled. "You'll shoot me dead anyway."

I nodded. "Probably. But at least not until we've had a chance to clear some other stuff up."

"And what makes you think I'll comply?"

"Ego."

Benny wiped his mouth. "Can't we just kill her and go?"

"Not yet. We need to find the flash memory card that Joey had on him. They took it when they killed him and supposedly they made a back-up of it. We can't leave without destroying that information."

"Yes we can," said Benny.

I glanced at him. "Why?"

"The information was fake."

I shook my head. "I saw some of it. I recognized a few names on it."

Benny smiled. "Niles put some real stuff on there mixed in with 99% bogus material. There's nothing on there worth tracking down and destroying."

I frowned. "What about the real names?"

"What about them? According to Niles, they're guys close to retirement anyway."

I thought about it. It would be a lot easier to simply shoot

Miranda and go. But then again, what if my name had been on that flash drive? What if I'd been close to retiring and some Control decided it would be worth sacrificing me in order to shut down a band of bad guys? Nothing like coming home one night and finding a kill team waiting for you.

"We're not leaving."

Benny sighed. "Dammit, Lawson, she's got other guys back there. At least ten of them. And all of them have a lot more guns than we do, which at last count was exactly one. And I ain't exactly spry enough to run and evade these dudes, dude."

I looked at Miranda who seemed to be taking all of this in stride. "Where's the data backed up?"

"I'm not going to tell you."

I nodded and checked to make sure the hammer was still back. "I'll count to three. At which time, I will put two rounds into that bizarrely braided head of yours and leave your corpse to the rats."

Miranda's eyebrows jumped. "You don't like my braids?"

I frowned. "Looks weird. But that doesn't matter-"

"It matters to me."

I nodded. "Great. Whatever. One."

Miranda brought her hands up to the back of her head. "I mean, I can certainly change things if you'd prefer."

"Two-"

She smiled again. "After all, I do enjoy looking my best when I have such esteemed guests in my house."

She ripped the braids from her head so suddenly, I scarcely had time to register the act. I caught the whiff of blood on the air from where Miranda had torn her own hair out.

I glanced at the floor and saw the braids laying there, one end of each a bloody mass of hair.

No.

Not hair.
As I watched, the braids shifted.
Squirmed.
And started to move.
Toward us.

17

"What the hell-?"

I could tell from the tone of Benny's voice that he was a little bit freaked out. So was I. I'm not used to people tearing the hair out and then watching as that hair transforms itself into something...else.

Snakes?

No.

As I watched the squirming masses mutate and lengthen, hundreds of tiny legs sprouted from either side, along with two long antennae. The creatures buzzed along the ground and I heard the click-clack of what must have been rows of razor sharp teeth.

Miranda clucked. "Oh, my babies are hungry."

"Lawson..."

I glanced at Benny. One of the giant carnivorous centipedes was heading straight at him.

I shot it.

The roar of the gun stopped the other bugs from moving. The wooden-tipped bullet tore into the first bug, spraying the floor and wall with bits of legs, flesh, and blood.

"No!" Miranda's shriek echoed off the walls. She frowned and lifted her hands toward Benny and me.

The centipedes came for us.

I wasn't crazy about shooting them. I only had so many rounds in the gun, and Miranda's reinforcements, while noticeably absent, were still a consideration. Perhaps they'd seen enough of the mutant centipedes to not want to get involved.

I didn't blame them.

Benny had another bug closing in on him. I sidestepped the corpse of the first one and brought my foot down on the back of the second. There was the slightest bit of hesitation before the back of the bug gave and gravity exerted its full effect.

The bug's body gooshed under my foot.

Benny blanched and I wondered if he was going to puke again.

"Lawson!"

I felt the impact just as I started to turn. The last centipede had somehow leaped on to my back. I could feel the probing antenna dancing over the skin of my neck as its feet scrambled up my back.

The sound of its teeth was far too close for comfort.

I tried to reach it with my hands, but it kept to my spine.

"Get it off of me!"

Benny spun me around but I could see there was just no way he was going to be able to convince himself that reaching for the bug with his hands was a good idea.

"Benny!"

The antennae brushed into my hair. I could hear the clicking of the teeth now closer than ever. Any moment I expected them to clamp down on my neck, adding my own bloody gore to the paint job.

Benny spun me around until he faced me. His eyes looked sad.

"I'm sorry!"

Then with all of his weight, he rushed me straight back into the wall.

The bug on my back exploded – trapped between me and the wall – as Benny rushed us into it. I felt a cascade of warmth run down my back. The probing antennae went still, but remained in my hair. I plucked them out and tossed them down onto the floor where they twitched once and then lay still.

The room stunk of fetid cheese and copper blood.

I didn't even want to know what my back looked like.

"My babies..."

I looked up at Miranda. "I'm asking myself if I even want to know how you managed to create such things."

She glanced up at me, tears running out from beneath her sunglasses. "I genetically altered them to increase their size and appetite."

"And they lived in your head?"

"On my head."

"And they fed on...?"

"Flesh. Mostly pigs and chickens. But vampire or human flesh would do in a pinch. They prefer brains though."

"Well, who wouldn't?"

Benny threw up one final time for good measure, adding to the already overpowering aroma in the room. I barely glanced at him and shook my head. "Thanks."

"Can't help it."

I kept my gun trained on Miranda. "All right. Enough of this. It's time for you to hand over the data I want and we'll be on our way."

She shook her head. "I can't do that."

I thumbed the hammer back again. "I won't ask you again."

She smiled. "Do I look like I'm begging for my life?"

"Fair enough."

I fired.

Miranda vanished.

In the close confines of the room, the shell that ejected from the gun spun and bounced and clinked to a stop in the corner of the room. I sniffed the cordite and found it a welcome relief from the pukish bloody scent that hung heavy in the air.

"What the hell?"

Benny was next to me. "Where the fuck did she go?"

The room was empty.

I stooped and looked under the table, almost convincing myself that Miranda might have the ability to somehow make herself tiny and fit under it.

But she wasn't there.

Benny wandered across the room to the wall opposite us. He brushed his fingers against the plaster and held them up. "Powder residue and bullet fragments."

"So, the gun works."

"Yeah, but it didn't hit anything."

"She was here."

Benny nodded. "I know. But now she ain't, dude."

I heard laughing then, a low steady cackle that grew in intensity until my head throbbed with the sound of it.

The lights went out in the room.

"Welcome to my world, Lawson."

18

"Lawson?"

I wanted to cuff Benny across the head for making noise in the absolute darkness that had flooded the room. But I knew that by doing so, I'd be giving my position away.

Unless Miranda already knew where I was.

A vague hissing filled the room. I still had the gun and swiveled toward the sound, unsure if I should fire or not. Something inside me said no and I stopped my trigger finger from taking up the slack on the gun.

Miranda's voice seemed to float above us and all around us. "It's so nice when you can't see your surroundings in the darkness but I can see splendidly."

I frowned. Where the hell was she?

Benny had shut up, which was a good sign. I strained my eyes trying to make out anything that I might use to my advantage.

But when I felt something cold and clammy slam into me and knock the gun away, I knew my life was about to get a lot worse. I listened to the pistol go clattering away into the darkness and in the next instant, something wrapped itself around me.

Squeezing.

The hiss was in my ear then. "So nice to see you again, Lawson..."

I grunted. "Miranda?"

"The same my dear. Tell me, how do you like the sweet sensation of being squeezed slowly to death?"

"You're a...snake?"

"What's the matter? Don't you enjoy mythology?"

I took a shallow breath. "I never knew Gorgons existed."

"They don't. But I'm a sucker for trying to create my own spin on the legends of early man. I'm a bit of a humanophile, I guess."

Yeah, so am I, but I usually limit myself to seducing human women. Now I was wrapped up by a freak who enjoyed tampering with genetics and turning herself into supernatural creatures.

Just my luck.

I worked my hands free and beat down against what felt like a tremendously thick rubber hose wrapped around my waist. My strikes seemed to have no effect whatsoever.

"I'm quite impervious to your measly attacks now that you don't have your precious pistol."

I could feel the coils working their way higher. Miranda was going for my ribs and if she succeeded, she'd squeeze the air right out of my lungs and probably make my heart pop at the same time. None of which sounded like the promising future I'd always envisioned for myself.

I sensed movement and thrust my hands out into the darkness, grabbing Miranda's head. She laughed.

"Are you sure you want to do that?"

Instantly, I felt smaller coils wrap themselves around my hands and wrists. The slithering creatures worked their way up my arms as Miranda's thicker coils worked their way higher on my body.

Breathing was getting tough.

My air came in short gasps as I tried to make my inhalations and exhalations as tight as possible, giving Miranda little room to tighten down on.

It wasn't working.

Every time I took a breath, I paid dearly for it.

"You're running out of precious seconds, Lawson." Every word she spoke accentuated the hiss. I expected her forked tongue to French kiss me at any moment.

"Shouldn't you be molting somewhere?"

She laughed again and squeezed tighter.

I grunted. Miranda apparently didn't appreciate my attempts at humor.

I could hear Benny scrambling in the darkness, breathing hard. Was he battling his own giant snake? Had the centipedes come back to life?

"Benny!"

"I can't find the damned thing, Lawson. I can't find it!"

What the hell was he looking for? I frowned. My pistol. It had to be. Benny knew there'd be no way for me to break free unless he found my pistol and shot Miranda.

"Get the damned lights!"

Miranda's voice was soft in my ear as the smaller coils threaded their way up past my biceps. "No need, sweetest. I'll take care of that."

Bright light flooded the room. I clamped my eyes shut, wincing as I did so.

Benny cried out.

I risked a look.

Miranda's body had morphed into a gigantic python with brown speckled spots and veins of gold twisting through her body. Her head was the only thing that remained vaguely humanoid, but she'd sprouted new locks – smaller snakes that wriggled and writhed as they squirmed up my arms.

I was locked close into Miranda's body – she had wrapped herself around me, each coil undulating like an iindependent sentient being. The smaller snakes kept my hands fastened to Miranda's head.

Benny pointed. "What the hell, dude…"

My breath came even shorter now. I choked out, "The gun…" and then had to try and suck wind into me just to keep from passing out.

Miranda's head bobbed back and forth. "Any time now, my sweet Fixer and you will belong to me. I shall so enjoy swallowing you whole and digesting you over the next few weeks."

My vision started to blur. A line of sweat broke out along my hairline. My tongue felt thick and mossy as I tried to croak another breath into my lungs. I only wanted a little air, just a little. But every time I tried, Miranda's coils snugged themselves even tighter around my body.

I cold feel the bones starting to rub against each other. Already it felt like my ribs had been kicked in hard. Several of them were probably broken. Sleeping, if I made it out of this thing alive, would be a real bitch for the next few weeks.

I sensed movement, but things were too hazy to discern what exactly was happening.

Benny?

More snakes?

I was losing consciousness. Blackness seemed to be creeping up on me and there wasn't a damned thing I could do about it.

Death by giant freakish snake didn't sound like a good epitath. I hoped Niles would write a better one.

Maybe even invite Talya.

I was already fading out when I heard the gunshot on the very fringes of my conscious mind.

19

The pressure released.

And I sucked air into my lungs as the my vision returned.

Benny stood in the corner of the room still holding the gun aimed at Miranda's slimy body. He looked close to shock.

"You okay?"

He nodded. "I've never shot a gun before."

I stepped over the coils. "Well, allow me to be the first to say that you picked one really spectacular time to start."

He grinned. "You all right, dude?"

I rubbed my left side and grimaced. "Tender, but possibly not broken. I'll pass judgment later tonight when I finally get some freaking sleep."

Benny pointed at Miranda's corpse, which had been torn apart by the single shot, spraying the floor and walls with bloody gore. "Can we leave now?"

I shook my head. "We're not leaving until we get all that information. Or did you forget?"

"I was hoping you would."

"Not a chance." I took the gun from him and led the way to

the door. I listened and could hear nothing on the other side. I took a breath and turned the door knob.

The room emptied into another hallway. At the far end, there were two doors, one of which was marked EXIT. I nodded and watched as Benny's eyes caught the word. He smiled and we moved on.

Surprisingly, Benny was decent at moving quietly. When this was all over, I was going to have to find out how he and Niles had hooked up and how in the world Benny had gotten involved in all of this crap.

But right now...

We got close to the second door and again, I paused to listen. Nothing.

I frowned. What the hell had happened to all of Miranda's henchmen? I thought I'd counted at least six of them. I glanced at Benny and shrugged. No sense arguing with a lack of bad guys.

I kept the pistol in low-ready, aiming just below the horizon as I entered and cleared left to right.

"Jesus."

Benny came in behind me and brought a hand up to his mouth. "What the hell, dude?"

We'd found Miranda's henchmen. All eight of them were draped across bits of furniture and on the floor. I checked the ones closest to me and looked at Benny. "Dead?"

He nodded. "All of them."

"What the hell happened here?"

Benny hauled one of the corpses off a computer terminal and sat down. With a few quick keystrokes, he brought up several screens of information. "It's here."

I came over. "All of it?"

Benny nodded. "And it hasn't been downloaded."

"So Miranda was lying about the offsite facility having backup copies of the data."

"Sure looks that way."

"Good." I calpped him on the back. "Make it go away. All of it. I don't want anything left behind that could compromise anyone."

"Good as done," said Benny. I watched him stroke the keys like a master pianist and within seconds he leaned back and stretched his hands back overhead.

"That was fast."

He grinned. "Hey, you do your thing. I do mine. Impressively, I might add."

I glanced around the room. Along with an assortment of weapons, I noticed a well-worn machete laying near a coconut that hadn't been split. Judging by the position of the body nearest it, that had been the plan.

"What do you think happened here?"

Benny shook his head. "No idea."

I glanced back. "There anything else on that computer?"

Benny hovered over the keys. "Bunch of files. Looks like some fairly elaborate graphs or tables or something."

I walked over. "Miranda mentioned she was into tampering with genetics. Maybe that's her research?"

"Could be." Benny hit the keys again and the screen buzzed full of junk.

None of it looked like scientific research.

Benny pointed. "Hey dude, those are like ancient glyphs and shit." He used the mouse to scroll down. "And those are scans of woodblock cuttings. Check that out."

I was. As Benny used his mouse to pore through the material contained on the computer, I scanned along with him. "That's not exactly what I expected to find on this thing."

Benny sighed. "Wish I had a way of pulling this off and taking it with us."

"No flash drives handy, huh?"

He shook his head. "No."

That was a shame. I would have loved getting this material to my friend Wirek back in Boston. He was an Elder, someone schooled in preserving the wisdom of the vampire race. He knew a helluva lot about ancient rituals, the traditions, and even bits of magical knowledge supposedly long lost in modern times.

But no dice without a mean of preserving the data.

"I don't suppose you feel like humping that desktop back to Boston, huh?"

Benny looked at me like I had three heads. "After I just saved your ass? Are you crazy?"

"Just figured I'd ask. See if you felt like taking one for the team."

Benny pointed at the screen. "You know, if Miranda told you she was into genetics, then this doesn't make any sense. This ain't genetic information at all, near as I can figure it."

I nodded. "That what has me worried, too."

"Seems obvious she lied."

"Yeah." I looked around the room. "And she had a bunch of guys here who obviously were not expecting to die any time soon. So what gives? How does this all tie in?"

"They died so I might live."

I spun, bringing up the gun.

Miranda stood in the doorway, her arms outstretched.

I felt a tug, then a yank.

My gun flew away from me.

And Miranda just laughed.

20

Out of the corner of my eye, I saw Benny rush right at Miranda. For someone as large as he was, he managed to get himself moving.

Unfortunately, Miranda merely flicked a hand at him and he went sailing back into the wall, leaving a huge depression in the plaster. He slid to the floor unconscious.

"Always so troublesome." Miranda clucked twice and then turned back to me. "And you, Fixer, have very obviously overstayed your welcome on this plane of existence."

She started to lower her glasses.

I looked away.

She laughed. "It's useless to refuse me, Lawson. I know there's a huge part of you that is desperate to know what it's like to look into my eyes. You want to see what the others have seen."

I kept my eyes on the ground.

"There are secrets within me – secrets you can know. Imagine what you'll discover. All it takes is one little glance. Just one."

I backed up, shaking my head. I was still winded from the

deadly squeeze Miranda had tried to put on me. "How did you do it?"

She laughed again and I was truly getting tired of listening to it. "I'm sure you've figured out it wasn't genetics at all."

"Magic."

"Old magic," said Miranda. "The kind most of our people have disdained for many years. It's lain dusty and tarnished. But it has always waited for the right person to come along and blow it off."

Miranda advanced on me. I kept backing up.

"I'm not the only one, Lawson. There are others like me. Right his very moment, they are resurrecting the old ways and adding to their own power. Who knows? Perhaps, there will come a time when even the likes of Fixers will not be enough to stop us."

"You'll all die."

"I think not. How can we die, when we have the power over life and death?"

In my peripheral vision I could see Miranda shifting to my left. With my hands behind me, guiding me, I kept moving.

"You obviously need the living to come back from the dead."

"You mean these fools?" She sighed. "It's true. I was able to resurrect myself by robbing them of their souls. I like to believe they would have gladly volunteered them in the interest of keeping me alive."

"I'm sure. But not everyone will be so forthcoming."

"What we can't get my guile, we'll take by force."

"You seem comfortable with that philosophy."

"Why wouldn't I be? It's how I've lived every moment of my life thus far. I don't intend to change now."

My hands brushed one of the tables. I backed into it, and moved to the right, my hands still guiding me.

Miranda circled around, trying to draw down the distance

between us. "You can't run from me all night, Lawson. Sooner or later you are going to get tired."

"I'm already exhausted."

"So why not simply give in? I promise you it won't be like that fool Jorell. I'll make it fast. I can do that you know. Make it fast. Painless even. All you have to do is look into my eyes."

"Surrender's not a concept I do well with."

Benny hadn't moved, so I wasn't going to get any help from him. My hands brushed over some pieces of something rope-like that I couldn't figure out what it was.

"It's not surrender, Lawson. It's giving in to the inevitable. Some might even say it was honorable to choose this way to go out."

"Cowards would say that."

She moved faster then, and in an instant, the space between us was cut to just eight feet. I was running out of room. I was out of ideas.

And I was totally out of energy.

"One look."

I backed up one more time. My hands scrambled over something sharp.

What-?

The coconut?

No.

Miranda rushed at me, her hands reaching to grab my shoulders and hold me in place while she gave me her death stare.

Instead, I let my hands clamp down over the machete and side-stepped as Miranda came rushing in.

She flew past me.

I spun clockwise, desperately trying to generate the necessary momentum.

I whipped the machete blade at the back of her neck.

It bit into her flesh and kept going, cleaving through her

spinal cord, tearing through her tendons and arteries, chopping her trachea and then slicing through the final flap of skin.

Miranda's head sailed off of her body.

A fountain of blood erupted and sprayed the ceiling as her body sank to its knees and then toppled over on the floor.

I heard a final gasp escape her lips from somewhere off in a corner of the room.

She was dead.

And this time, there'd be no way to rob anyone of their soul and come back to life.

I leaned against the table and let the machete blade slide to the floor into the expanding pool of blood that was making the floor slick.

But damn, needed a vacation.

EPILOGUE

Manila International Airport never looked so good.

"Sure you won't come home?"

I looked at Benny who sported a fresh bandage over his head from the skull lacerations he'd gotten courtesy of Miranda. We stood at the crossroads. One terminal led to Europe and American destinations. The other led to other destinations in the Far East.

"I've got to go," I said. "I've needed this vacation more than any other I've ever taken."

"How many have you taken before?"

"Counting this one? Exactly one."

He smiled. "Always knew you were a workaholic."

"Yeah, well, it's not always easy taking a trip when you've got a pest of a Control who keeps calling you to run errands for him."

Benny touched his head. "Yeah, he promised me no action when this all started."

"Never believe that." I smiled. "How did he find you anyway?"

Benny shook his head. "Would you believe he came to my

place? Knocked on my door one day, said he was a friend of yours-"

"Your first mistake. You know I don't have any friends."

Benny made his eyes go droopy. "Not even me?"

"Well, I do have a few other rogues who seem to be able to stand my presence."

"Yeah, well Niles digs you. He said he had a job proposal for me and was I interested in helping you out of a jam."

"And you jumped at the chance, right?"

Benny shook his head. "Nah, he had to bribe me first with promises of women and money."

"Good to know I rate so highly."

"Niles explained the Loyalist thing to me."

"And you're cool with the whole..."

"Vampire thing?" he shrugged. "I guess. I mean, what the hell right? Like we don't know everything that goes on around the world? I've never thought humans were the only race of sentient beings this place has."

"That's mighty open minded of you."

"Yeah, plus it totally stokes my geek streak, dude. Just a shame I can't trumpet it on the Net, you know?"

"Um, yeah, please don't."

Benny set his luggage down and sighed. "Niles had me create the list and then arrange for Joey to carry it over while I flew another flight."

"Joey a friend of yours?"

Benny smiled. "Dude, he owed me like fifty grand in unpaid expenses. I'm not shedding a tear over his demise, lemme tell you."

"Okay."

"Niles had me come in as the leak, meet with Jorell and his gang and offer you up."

"And all of this was to get to Miranda?"

"According to what Niles told me, they knew there was a criminal organization getting ready to expand into the US. They wanted them taken out before they got the chance to do that."

I frowned. "So Niles had no idea what Miranda actually was?"

"I doubt it."

I clapped him on the back. "You're going to have some debrief, pal. Wish I could be there to see his eyes when you tell him."

"Yeah, well I missed the best part – you cleaving her head off with a machete. Very Greek mythology of you, dude."

"There will be no discussion of me wearing loin cloths when I get back."

Benny laughed.

I looked at my ticket. "Time to go."

Benny grabbed my hand and pumped it a few times. "You take care in Japan. And if you need anything, just call."

"I will."

Benny hefted his luggage. "See ya."

I watched him trundle down the concourse. He seemed a lot lighter on his feet than I remembered. Maybe it was the fact that he knew something most other people didn't. Benny always loved knowing secrets. And now he knew one of the biggest secrets of all.

I hoped he didn't ever tell anyone.

That would mean a visit from me.

I shook my head. Benny was a good guy. And I was lucky to have had him along on this venture.

I grabbed my bag and walked down to the ticket counter. The attractive young woman at the Japan Air Lines counter greeted me with a big smile. She punched the keys in front of her and then handed me my ticket back.

"Have a pleasant flight, Mr. Lawson."

I resisted the urge to flirt and smiled at her instead. "Thank you."

Ahead of me, the security gate waited.

Beyond that, a trip to the land of the rising sun.

And hopefully...a lot of rest.

REVIEWS

If you've enjoyed this book, I sincerely hope you'll leave a great review over on Amazon. Reviews are critical to the success of an author and even a few lines (or no lines at all, just stars) helps propel the book into Amazon's marketing algorithms.

ABOUT THE AUTHOR

Jon F. Merz is the author of over 40 novels ranging from urban fantasy to espionage and sword & sorcery fantasy. Prior to becoming a full-time writer Jon served in the United States Air Force, protected a variety of Fortune 500 executives, and taught defensive tactics to government agencies like the State Department, Bureau of Prisons, and others. He is an active CrossFitter, a 5th degree black belt in Togakure-ryu Ninjutsu, enjoys doing GORUCK challenges, and in 2014 started modeling and acting in television commercials. He lives each and every day by the motto, "Who Dares Lives." He and his wife Joyce (who runs the hugely popular food blog **The Tasty Page**) live with their two sons in suburban Boston.

Connect with Jon!
www.jonfmerz.net
jonfmerz@gmail.com

THE LAWSON VAMPIRE SERIES

1. The Fixer: A Lawson Vampire Novel
2. The Invoker: A Lawson Vampire Novel
3. The Destructor: A Lawson Vampire Novel
4. The Syndicate: A Lawson Vampire Novel
5. The Price of a Good Drink: A Lawson Vampire Story
6. The Courier: A Lawson Vampire Mission
7. The Kensei: A Lawson Vampire Novel
8. Enemy Mine: A Lawson Vampire Story
9. The Ripper: A Lawson Vampire Novel
10. Rudolf The Red Nosed Rogue: A Lawson Vampire Story
11. Interlude: A Lawson Vampire Story
12. The Shepherd: A Lawson Vampire Mission
13. Red Tide: A Lawson Vampire Story
14. Frosty The Hitman: A Lawson Vampire Story
15. A Fog Of Fury: A Lawson Vampire Mission
16. Invitation to Dance: A Lawson Vampire Story
17. The Crucible: A Lawson Vampire Novel
18. Oathbreaker: A Lawson Vampire Story
19. Do You Kill What I Kill? A Lawson Vampire Story
20. Incident at Palmyra: A Lawson Vampire Mission

21. Lady of the Dead: A Lawson Vampire Mission
22. A Forced Disappearance: A Lawson Vampire Mission
23. Here Comes Santa Claus: A Lawson Vampire Story
24. The Succubus: A Lawson Vampire Novel
25. The Koryo Escort: A Lawson Vampire Mission
26. Daughter of Night: A Lawson Vampire Mission

THE LAWSON VAMPIRE ORIGINS SERIES

1. Dead Drop: A Lawson Vampire Origins Story
2. The Enchanter: A Lawson Vampire Origins Novel
3. The Cairo Connection: A Lawson Vampire Origins Mission
4. Mission: Malta: A Lawson Vampire Origins Mission
5. Have Yourself A Deadly Little Christmas: A Lawson Vampire Origins Story
6. The Infiltrator: A Lawson Vampire Origins Mission
7. Killing Around The Christmas Tree: A Lawson Vampire Origins Story
8. Ghost In The Machine: A Lawson Vampire Origins Story
9. The Snitch Who Stole Christmas: A Lawson Vampire Origins Story

Made in United States
Orlando, FL
20 March 2022